Devious

A Jamie Richmond Mystery

Mark Love

Devious
Copyright © 2015 Mark Love
All rights reserved.

ISBN: (ebook) 978-1-939590-66-4
(Print) 978-1-939590-61-9

Inkspell Publishing
5764 Woodbine Ave.
Pinckney, MI 48169

Edited By David Hayes
Cover art By Dawne' Dominique

DEDICATION

For Kim, who has always been there to remind me that the
journey can be as important as the destination.

MARK LOVE

PROLOGUE

I can't believe I'm standing here with a gun in my hand. And it's pointed at his chest. My heart's pounding in such a pronounced manner you'd think I had just run five miles. But there's anger mixed with the adrenalin coursing through my system.

If someone told me four months ago I'd be facing a life or death situation, I would have gotten them a nice cup of tea and tried to find some way to calm them down before the ambulance arrived to carry them away. Danger is not my forte. I don't live for danger. I live vicariously, documenting the courage and exploits of others. The scariest thing I have ever done is eat yogurt after the expiration date.

But now here I stand, gripping a weapon and praying I won't have to use it as he narrows the gap between us. Yet, despite my hammering heart, I realize there is no way this ends neatly. There is too much at stake. I've already had a visit with Death tonight, and it wasn't pleasant. Can I take the shot? Or will he rip it away from me and kill me with my own gun?

How could this be happening to me?

CHAPTER ONE

It seems sudden death always brings us together. Amid the noise and confusion, I sensed his presence. Over there, behind the blinding flashes of colored light. Despite the pulsating crowd of spectators, despite the noise and the confusion, I saw *him*.

And he saw me.

He stood impassively, muscular chest straining to be contained inside his jacket. Even the sleeves were stretched to capacity. There was a scowl on his face. Perhaps it was a look of disgust, or maybe defiance. His eyes narrowed when they registered my own. If I had been expecting any acknowledgement, I was going to be disappointed. He turned his back on me and disappeared behind the lights.

I turned away, shaking my head.

* * * *

It was three days later before he agreed to see me. Despite the appointment I made, he kept me waiting fifteen minutes. At last the door opened. He waved me inside, closing off the escape route firmly behind me.

There was that awkward moment when neither one of us knew exactly what to do. Finally, with a snort that could have either been disgust or laughter, he drew me close for a bear hug.

"You look good, Jamie."

"You too, Bert. Still working out?"

"Every chance I get. How's Vera?"

I tensed at the mention of her name. With his arm still around me, I had no doubt that he could feel it.

"She's good."

"Still with that psychiatrist?"

I shook my head. "No way, that was a year ago. She's two beyond that. First there was a lawyer, now a stockbroker."

"Sounds like crooks to me, just fancier versions." He waved me to a chair in front of his desk.

"I still think you were her favorite, although it may have been a close race between you and the plastic surgeon." He snorted again and shook his head.

Sometimes it's hard for me to think of Bert as my father. Technically, he was, or is, my stepfather. He was my mother's third husband. The first, Peter Richmond, was an artist. His sculptures still decorate several local galleries and museums. He had just been hitting his stride, having done a number of successful commercial projects, when a fall from scaffolding suddenly ended his career. That his life also ended then seemed secondary to my mother. I was seven at the time.

She has progressed her way through a number of romances and marriages, trying to find the right combination of husband—lover. Bert married her when I was thirteen. She divorced him when I was twenty. She was currently on her seventh husband. I'd lost count of the boyfriends in between or during the other marriages. I'd never say it to her face, but she has developed a severe Mrs. Robinson complex. Her last three lovers were half her age.

Albert "Bert" Nowalski dressed more like a businessman than a police captain. And maybe, nowadays, that's what was necessary. His tailored suit, freshly pressed, probably cost more than two weeks' pay. He favored Italian shoes that were always gleaming with polish, and starched white shirts so crisp they looked brand new. He still wore the expensive Swiss watch Vera had given him as a wedding present. If you hinted that he was sentimental, he'd counter that it was merely an excellent timepiece that fit well. Bert always kept his hair short, in a crew cut style that was barely more than stubble. His piercing gray eyes never missed a trick, something I'd learned the hard way during my teenage years.

"Why were you hanging out at that crime scene Friday night? I thought you'd given up the police beat for something more normal." He settled into the chair behind his desk.

After several years working for one of the local daily papers, I decided to take matters into my own hands. I'd started out with society and fashion, then gradually worked my way into where my real interest lies. Crime. I covered everything from the scenes, to arraignments and to trials. Along the way, I had a scare or two; this made me want to work on my own terms. Now, I write features that appeal to me and sell them to magazines all over the country. Sometimes, I can put a new slant on the same article and sell it to half a dozen different 'specialty' magazines. This allows me time to set my own schedule and to work on what I really want to do—write mysteries.

I've done features on acrobats, gourmet chefs, successful businesswomen, construction workers, motorcycle riding nuns and a judge who was blind and used a guide dog to help him navigate his way, even in the courtroom. There have been stories about new rock bands, musical prodigies under the age of ten and a dyslexic spelling bee champ. Now, it was time for something new. I'd hoped that my relationship with Bert, whatever that currently was, would give me the inside track.

"It was just force of habit. I was driving by and saw the lights. Guess I'm still a reporter at heart. If there was enough for a complete story, I could have covered it and sold the effort to my old editor."

"So why didn't you follow it up?" Bert asked.

"By the time I asked a few questions, I realized two other stringers had beaten me to the punch. They must have heard the calls on the scanner. I gave mine up when I wanted to focus on features."

"Good for you. I never liked the idea of you digging into the crime beat."

"You meet some of the most interesting people that way," I said with a smile.

"Too bad some of those 'interesting people' are lacking in table manners." Bert rocked slowly in his chair. He was as comfortable in his surroundings as I am at home. "So, why are you here, Jay? You want to take one of your many stepfathers out to lunch?"

"Technically, I only have two steps: you and Renaldo. And I wouldn't waste the price of a Whopper on him."

Bert snorted his laugh again. "Renaldo. There's a joker I hadn't thought about in years. Wasn't he selling time shares or something?"

I nodded. "Last we heard from him, he was working on the ocean in South Carolina. Right before the hurricane ripped through."

"I recall when you were fifteen and went through a phase where you were going to be a vegetarian. That lasted until I was grilling steaks." He grinned at the memory and gave his head a slow shake. "Level with me, Taffy Ass. Why are you here?"

"Taffy ass? I haven't heard that in years. I keep hoping you'd forgotten that by now."

"Not on your life. That was one of the funniest things I've ever seen."

Maybe to him, but to me, it was one of my most

embarrassing moments ever. It happened when I was sixteen. There was a dance at school and I had gone with a group of kids. It wasn't an official date. But Nicky Valenti had been very attentive that night. He bought me a Coke and a slice of pizza. We shared a few slow dances. Nicky was a senior. All the girls thought he was charming, with a sly smile and soulful brown eyes. I was junior. He had borrowed the keys to a friend's car.

On the way out to the parking lot to 'look at the stars', he'd bought me a few pieces of taffy. I was young. I was naïve. I slid them into the back pocket of my jeans. After an hour of passionate kissing in the backseat of the car, we returned to the dance. The taffy had melted through my pocket, staining my jeans, my underwear and my bottom. My face was as red as my hair when I tried to explain it away to Vera. Bert didn't believe a word of the story I came up with that night, and had tagged me taffy ass. He only used it in private and always with impeccable timing.

I couldn't con him. He was far too sharp to accept anything but the truth. "I'm working on a mystery. I finally sold a book. It'll be published in the spring."

A wide smile split his face. "That's great! Why didn't you tell me?"

I blushed at his enthusiasm. "I don't want to jinx it. Until I see the actual book in my hands, I keep thinking something will go wrong. Like a bad blind date."

.Jay, I've told you a hundred times, you've got talent. I said that back when you were working on the paper in high school."

Bert always encouraged me. It's nice to see some things never change.

"They offered me an advance on a second book, and I want one of my key characters to be a patrol officer. I'd like to ride a shift or two with a uniformed trooper."

"The state police force is not in the habit of allowing civilians to patrol with a trooper. Your presence could interfere with the performance of his duties." Bert was trying hard to keep the twinkle out of his eye. For a moment, he almost had me fooled.

"Surely there must be exceptions to every policy, Captain, even in police work." I tried to think of something to bargain with.

He chuckled and stopped rocking. "Don't get formal on me, little girl. Remember, I'm the one who caught you climbing up the trellis after curfew when you first discovered boys."

"Hey, I was fifteen. And that's ancient history, like a dozen years ago."

The twinkle was definitely there. "Sixteen. But who's counting. Anyway, I didn't say we wouldn't allow it. I'm just not so sure it would be a good idea. Things are a little tense among the troopers, with the governor spouting off about budget reform for the new fiscal year."

I knew what he meant. The latest political savior had some unorthodox ideas on attempting to balance the state's budget. Radical changes in the number of state troopers were only one of the methods currently being considered.

"What are you suggesting, Bert?"

"Best time for you to witness would be a daylight watch. Things aren't nearly as hectic as when the sun goes down."

I leaned forward, trying to read his expression. Nothing. Even as a kid, I could never gain any insight from his face. "If it's all the same to you, I'd much rather take an evening shift."

Bert shook his head and closed his eyes. "You're not going to make this easy for me, are you, Jay?"

"C'mon, Bert, have a heart. I'm talking about one shift, in the evening, with a regular trooper. Eight hours and I'm out of your hair. And I'll never mention to Vera that I saw you, or how good you look." It was a shot, but I knew deep down that he still cared about Vera, despite her numerous faults.

He paused, studying me with those cool eyes. I wish I could get a sense of what was going on behind them, but Bert still wouldn't give anything away. He'd tell me just enough when he was ready, and not before. At length, he slowly shook his head as if clearing his thoughts.

"Such flattery. You're a piece of work, Jamie Rae." He rocked again. "But I'd find it more amusing if you did mention it to your mother."

I hooked a thumb toward the rocking chair. "Nerves?"

He nodded once. "My therapist recommended it. Claims the relaxing motion of rocking could help me deal with the stress of the job. It ain't all traffic tickets and parades, you know."

I pounced on his comment. "No, I don't know. I only know the parts from the cases I've covered, which usually involved detectives. Which is precisely why I want, no, make that why I *need* to do this. So I can find out. It will make my story more realistic if I can show some of the real incidents that happen to a cop on patrol. Authentic background information is what I need for this book."

"Is there anyone not writing the Great American Novel?"

"Writing it is one thing. Getting it published is something else. C'mon, Bert. Say yes and I'll be your Valentine."

The face splitting smile returned. "I remember the first time you pulled that."

I came around the desk and planted a kiss on his cheek. "And who always sends you a card on Valentine's Day?"

"You do."

"And Christmas, Father's Day and your birthday?"

"You do."

"And who's your favorite stepdaughter?"

"You're my only stepdaughter."

"Doesn't that make me your favorite?"

"I guess it does."

"So you'll set it up?"

"Oh, all right," he said with just a hint of disgust. "I'll see to it. But if anything goes sour during the night, I'm giving the trooper specific orders to dump your taffy ass at the post."

"So are we clear? Any problems and they drop you at the post. Understood?"

I stood erect and snapped off a salute. "Understood."

Bert rose to escort me out to the lobby. I pulled a tissue out of my purse and carefully wiped the lipstick off his cheek. Bert was always fast on his feet, able to identify a problem and come up with a solution before I'd even finished speaking. I got the impression that I'd been snookered. He stopped me just outside his office, gently squeezing my elbow. "Why couldn't you do something safe, like teaching or modeling?"

I looked down at my chest. "I couldn't make it as a model. I'm lacking a few of the essentials."

"Bull. Legs like those could sell stockings. Hell, even I'd buy a pair." He gave me another brief hug then turned to go back to work.

"They call it hose now, Bert, pantyhose."

"Hey, I'm an old-fashioned guy. Besides, stockings sound a whole lot sexier than hose."

* * * *

Some people ask me why I choose to live in Michigan. There's a preconceived notion that all great writers must live in Los Angeles or New York. But I was born and raised here, and have grown to love the changing seasons and the cultural melting pot the Detroit area has to offer. There's a three-block section in downtown known as Greektown, where the best lamb in the country is served. There are Italian areas, Polish, Arab, Indian, Thai, Korean and Jewish. Even Japanese restaurants have sprung up lately.

Fall in southeastern Michigan always inspires me. It's

my favorite season. The leaves change color and cover the yards everywhere with whirling patterns of red, orange and gold. The air turns cool and crisp. People are actually friendly toward one another. Apple orchards flourish, pumping out oceans of cider and caramel apples by the truckload. There's nothing like a freshly picked apple with the caramel still warm and covered with chopped nuts. It's a culinary bit of heaven. To celebrate my arrangement with Bert, I stopped at an orchard for a quart of cider and two caramel apples. Lunch, Michigan style. Then it was home to my waiting keyboard.

Two nights after our meeting he called me.

"Everything's arranged. Be at the station Friday by three o'clock."

"Friday night?" I hadn't expected to hear from him so soon.

"What's the matter? Got a date?" Bert taunted. "You wanted action, you'll get it. Friday's the busiest night on patrol."

"That's exactly what I want. Three o'clock is fine with me. Will you be there?"

"Sergeant Malone will be expecting you. You're his problem from roll call through the end of watch. And Jamie..."

"Yes?"

"Remember what I said, you stubborn redhead. If things get squirrelly…"

"My taffy ass will be dumped at the station."

"Just so long as we understand each other. No matter what anyone says, you're still my daughter. I don't care how old you are. And don't bother with that bull about being a stepdaughter."

I felt something catch in my throat. That was the first time he'd ever come right out with a statement like that. "I love you, Bert."

"Be good, Jamie."

It was almost as if he expected something bad to

happen.

CHAPTER TWO

I slept late Friday and rushed about doing some errands. A pair of butterflies the size of Rhode Island did the mambo inside my stomach. Research can be exciting. I've traveled with a circus and walked the high wire (with a harness) during my last feature. Now, those memories seemed like a leisurely stroll compared to what lay ahead. Visions of high-speed chases, bullets flying, and sirens wailing all kept jumping through my mind. Was this really necessary? Maybe I could just hang out at a donut shop and eavesdrop on the conversations. But that would be cheating my audience as well as myself. I wanted this adventure.

On my way to the station I punched up the news channel on the car radio. I didn't like what I heard.

"Repeating the top story. Governor Aikens has announced his plan to cut staffing to the state police by twenty-eight percent next year. Despite protests from angry citizens and the troopers' union, the proposal has passed the state house. Layoffs will begin in January with the new fiscal year."

No wonder the governor had picked up the nickname

Axman. He'd already cut spending to support the arts, welfare, and unemployment. What a guy.

Parking behind the building, I tried to stop wondering how the cutbacks would affect the department and concentrate on my research. The troopers would have heard the news as well. My hopes of riding with a friendly cop who could give me plenty of insight into his daily routine might have vanished with the chop of the governor's cleaver.

Inside, I found Sergeant Malone to be a wiry man with frozen cobalt in his blue eyes, and a nose that had been broken more than once. I guessed him to be about five feet eleven inches tall, a good four inches above my own height. I also guessed he was about forty. Malone's hair was jet black and worn considerably longer than Bert's. He greeted me with genuine warmth and ushered me into a private office for a brief conversation.

"The captain left a message for you, Miss Richmond." He handed over a letter- sized envelope with the state emblem in the corner. I opened it and scanned the paper.

"What's this?"

"Standard release form. The department is willing to let you accompany a trooper during his patrol, but only if you waive any claims against the state, should anything happen to you during the evening. It's the normal procedure." Malone had a deep, gentle voice, almost sympathetic.

"What the hell." I signed the form, handing it back.

Malone returned the form to the envelope and placed it in a wire basket on his desk. I noticed how easily he handled the paperwork, and also the size of his hands. They looked strong.

"Now you're official."

I smiled softly. "What's the plan for the evening?"

He rested a hip against the edge of his desk. "The men don't know about you yet. It's easier to spring it on them without any warning. If we'd mentioned it earlier, there would be one of two scenarios. Either they'd all want you to ride with them, or they'd be trying to palm you off on a greenie."

"What's a greenie?"

Malone smiled. It was warm and low key and made his eyes dance. "Rookie. We've got two, fresh out of the academy, but they don't patrol alone." The smile faded. "If you heard the governor's latest budget announcement, you can figure those rookies won't be around for very long."

I nodded. "How many men do you expect to lose?"

"All told, maybe six. Most of our officers are veterans, seven years or more. It's the young guys who will get the axe. That's the shame, because when the older ones retire, who's going to be experienced enough to replace them?"

"Too bad the governor can't order a twenty-eight percent reduction in crime, to match his budget cuts," I said.

"Dream on." Malone took my elbow and guided me toward the door. "What do we call you?"

"Jamie will do. If you get real friendly, I'll let you call me Jay."

Malone led me to a large meeting room where the roll call would take place.

There was a lot of conversation going on as we entered. I sat at a long table next to the podium, and stared out at the troopers while Sergeant Malone went through the roll call. He informed them of their assignments, noted a series of burglaries occurring in Northville, and designated vehicles. Nobody mentioned the governor's announcement. I waited patiently, hands folded on the table before me. The evening shift was made up of two female officers, three black men, and four white men. Both women were white. I was glad I'd worn jeans and a sweater. This was neither the time nor the place for skirts and pantyhose.

Malone wrapped up his spiel then cast an eye about the room. The cops all shifted restlessly, eager to be on the road.

"Kleinschmidt. Front and center. The rest of you hit the streets. And like the man used to say, 'let's be careful out there'."

With a scuffling of chairs, the troopers left the conference room. Kleinschmidt waited until they were gone before coming forward. He was younger than most of the others. His body looked big but soft, as if he were out of condition. His hair was already receding rapidly toward the back of his skull.

"'Sup, Sarge?"

"This is Jamie Richmond," Malone said. "She's a reporter and an author. Tonight she's going to ride in your cruiser, observing your routine for research purposes. At no time is she allowed to interfere with the performance of your duties."

Kleinschmidt's full moon face fell. "An observer? Ah, c'mon Sarge. How about letting her ride with Billings or Rothman?"

"I don't want the lady bored to death with fishing stories. She wants to observe a regular trooper during his shift. That's you. End of discussion."

Kleinschmidt opened his mouth to argue his case but one good look from Malone changed his mind. Disgusted, he looked directly at me for the first time. "Okay, lady, let's go." He mumbled so softly, I almost didn't hear him. Malone followed us out to the parking area.

Kleinschmidt didn't offer to hold my door, which I appreciated. I was supposed to be an observer, not his date. He took a clipboard and filled in the upper half of a daily report. Name, badge number, rank, mileage on the car. He checked the lights, horn and emergency flasher. He shot a quick look at the tires. I glanced around for Malone. He was deep in conversation with a mechanic examining a patrol car. But his eyes met mine across the parking lot. He smiled another low-key flash of warmth. One of my butterflies did a back flip.

Kleinschmidt slid behind the wheel and keyed the

engine. "Ready, lady?"

I checked my safety belt. "Ready."

He put the car in gear and headed toward the freeway.

Trooper Kleinschmidt didn't talk to me for the first hour. Our assigned quadrant was a seven-mile stretch of the interstate, south and east of the post. Two main highways intersect the area, making for a lot of activity, especially during the commute home. Mass transportation and Detroit are terms that shouldn't be even remotely associated in the same sentence. Nearly everyone drives in the city. Carpooling is something people on the eastern seaboard might do. In Motown, it's every man, woman and child for themselves. And each of them in a separate car.

We cruised back and forth, rotating from north to south at whatever whim struck Kleinschmidt. I listened to the chatter on the radio and watched him. The patrol car was old, five or six years at least. The radar unit was inoperable. He floated the big Chevy from one lane to another, pacing cars occasionally. Traffic was already thick, and it wasn't even five o'clock yet. Boooooorrrrrrrring. His silence was getting on my nerves.

"I'm sorry if having a passenger offends you."

"Forget it, lady. My whole day has been going like this." Kleinschmidt cut the wheel and pulled alongside a delivery truck. He flashed his lights once, waiting until the driver reduced his speed. Then Kleinschmidt drove past and continued his patrol. The truck driver tooted his horn as we went by and I fought the urge to wave.

"No tickets?" I asked.

He shrugged. "It's hardly worth the trouble unless they're going seventy-five or faster. Truckers usually play it safe, but sometimes they need a little reminder." Kleinschmidt moved his hat from the dashboard and placed it gingerly on the seat between us.

"How long have you been on the force, officer?"

"Trooper. Three years. Thanks to Governor Axman's

plans, I don't think I'll get a fourth." His eyes flicked off the road for a second and he glanced at me. "What kind of things do you write?"

"Feature stories for newspapers and magazines. And I just sold a mystery novel. *Tightrope Twist.* Do you read mysteries, Trooper Kleinschmidt?"

His face softened for the first time. I could easily see him with a double chin in five years. "Call me Smitty. Sorry, I only read hunting magazines. Never been much of a bookworm."

I smiled. "Everybody's different. One thing I didn't ask Sgt. Malone, what do you do about dinner?"

"We get half an hour break for meals and two ten minute breaks for coffee. I usually don't stop until after nine. It makes the last part of the shift go by in a hurry. Okay with you, Miss Richmond?"

"Jamie. And nine o'clock is fine. Tonight's my treat. It's the least I can do, since you're stuck with me."

Smitty relaxed some more and rewarded me with an actual smile. "It's a deal."

It takes a certain type of person to be a cop. The majority of the population treats you like a rabid dog. Some show respect, but not many. People still have a hard time believing you're out there to help and protect them, not just to write tickets for speeding twenty miles an hour over the limit. A lot of people never think about it, me included.

Smitty stopped an old Mustang ten minutes later for an equipment failure. The front windshield was so badly cracked that I don't know how the kid could have possibly seen through it. Kleinschmidt gave him a ticket that would be waived if the car were repaired before the court date. He talked to the kid for a while about the vehicle in general and some bodywork the kid was going to do.

I'd gotten out of the car when he did, standing on the shoulder of the interstate. Cars and the occasional truck roared by. The backwash was enough to rock you in your tracks. I stayed out of the way, but got close enough to hear what was going on. In keeping with my role as an observer, I kept my mouth shut until we were back under way in the Chevy.

"What about the speeding? He was going pretty fast when you pulled him over."

"That's my call. The department gives us some leeway with traffic situations. He's just a kid. His record is clean. If I give him a verbal warning, it might be enough to slow him down a little. Besides, if I give him a break, he can afford to get that windshield fixed." Kleinschmidt didn't look at me as he continued down the road. He was more relaxed than when we'd left the post, but still all business.

Whenever Smitty left the car, his sunglasses remained behind and his hat was firmly in place. He approached each vehicle in the same manner, cautious, yet confident. Smitty turned as he walked, giving them only a profile of himself as he neared the driver's door. I asked him about it.

"Never boldly walk up to a car. It's a good way to get your head blown off. Anybody could be waiting there, with a gun in his hand, ready to kill you."

Ten minutes later he pulled over an old Camaro with expired license plates. Three large black women were squeezed inside. They kept sneaking looks out the rear window at me, trying to see what I was doing. Kleinschmidt came back to the unit, grumbling and shaking his head.

"What a mess. The driver has an expired license. Her sister, the front seat passenger, owns the car, but doesn't drive. The one in the back has no identification." Smitty stared at the car. All three women were now watching us.

"Do me a favor, Jamie."

"Sure."

"Stand right there and cross your arms, like you're mad at the world. Stare at them. Every once in a while, check your watch."

"Okay." I assumed the position he described.

"Perfect."

"What do you do now?"

"Call it in. See what the dispatcher can come up with. This could take a while to sort out." Kleinschmidt studied the car again then jerked his head in my direction.

I listened quietly while Smitty radioed in. He wasn't surprised when the results came back. Both sisters had warrants out for their arrests, stemming from the failure to appear in court. Now his job became even more difficult. While he was finishing up with the dispatcher, another patrol car pulled in behind us. A black trooper came over to join me at the hood. His nametag read Billings. He folded his arms across his chest and spoke out of the corner of his mouth.

"You, observer, what's going on?"

"Expired plates. Smitty's checking it out with the post." I caught myself talking out of the side of my own mouth. It seemed quite natural with my tough guy posturing.

"They want me to search the vehicle," Smitty said as he climbed out of the cruiser. "Keep standing where you are, Jamie, and try to look pissed off. Care to join in, Leo?"

Billings undid the snap that held his weapon in place. "Most definitely. I'll stand guard while you do the routine."

I did as he requested. The women wiggled out of the car and stood by the rear bumper, alternately watching me and Trooper Billings while Smitty searched the interior. Eventually they seemed to ignore Billings all together. There was a lot of nervous shuffling back and forth, but the trio was more interested in watching me watch them than in Smitty's search. Fifteen minutes passed before Kleinschmidt exited their car. He called the dispatcher, relayed the information, and got further instructions. He conferred with Billings then approached the trio.

At this point, the women had a choice. Pay a large cash bond to Kleinschmidt, or go to jail. I've heard stories about women keeping rolls of cash tucked in their bras, but this was the first time I actually saw anyone who did it. All three women got into the act. They dug out more money than a Vegas pit boss in ten seconds.

Kleinschmidt spent ten minutes doing the necessary paperwork for the cash bond and writing out tickets. Still using his best manners, he politely explained the situation.

"Okay ladies, here's the story. Your plates are expired, only one of you has a license, which is also expired, and you have no insurance. You have posted bond to allow you to remain free until your next court date. Here are the receipts. However, I suggest you do not drive this car until you have taken care of these infractions."

"How we gonna get home?" the driver asked.

"Call someone else for a ride. Or call a cab. It's your decision. I can't tell you what to do, but I suggest not driving this car."

She stamped her foot. "Shit."

Billings climbed into his cruiser and returned to his neighboring patrol area. Smitty waved me back into the car and we drove away. I looked over my shoulder to see the trio climbing back into the Camaro.

"They didn't even wait until you were out of sight," I said with a grin.

"Didn't think they would."

"What was all that about me standing there watching them?"

Smitty joined the flow of traffic before answering. "They kept asking about you, wondering why you were riding with me."

"Some people get a little weird when they meet a reporter," I said.

Kleinschmidt nodded and slid the car into one of those restricted areas of the median, where he casually spun the Chevy in the opposite direction.

"I didn't tell them you were a reporter."

"What did you tell them?"

He shrugged and refused to even glance at me for a

moment. "I said you were a narcotics cop. I told them you were riding with me until you got cleared from a shooting incident. Told them it probably wasn't your fault that pistol was locked on automatic."

CHAPTER THREE

It was dark by now, the late autumn sky pitch black. Even the stars and the moon were taking the night off. Smitty's attitude toward me softened after his stunt with the Camaro. He even grinned a few times and answered my questions openly, although briefly. Kleinschmidt was about to request a dinner break when the radio chirped to life.

"Twenty-one Brian. In pursuit of a red Mazda, headed west at Merriman. Traveling in excess of ninety miles per hour. Possible 54-2. Request assistance."

Smitty snagged the mike from the holder and keyed the button. "Twenty-one David two, responding E.T.A. thirty seconds."

"Roger, David two."

"What's a 54-2?" I asked as we roared off.

"Drunk driver. Better than seventy percent of all shootings involve alcohol. It's a priority to assist another officer when that code is called."

I stopped talking and braced my feet against the floorboards. Smitty mashed down the accelerator. The

Chevy raced along the road, sliding easily between the cars, blue lights twirling from the rooftop. My heart pounded frantically as if I were jogging alongside the car. My senses vibrated with excitement. I tried to absorb everything. The air in the Chevy no longer contained enough oxygen to suit me. In a flash, we had joined the high-speed chase.

I watched in amazement as three other patrol cars converged on the same spot. Somehow, one unit managed to get in front of the car while two others closed in from the sides. Smitty took the position directly behind the Mazda. The little red car swerved recklessly in an attempt to outmaneuver the police cars, but the troopers held their ground. With the speeder boxed in, they gradually reduced their speed until it was safe to force the car onto the shoulder of the freeway. My heart still thundered as if I'd run ten miles and my entire body was drenched with sweat.

"Wait here!" Smitty jumped out, the car not quite at a stop.

"Like hell," I muttered, scrambling out my door. He didn't look back, his attention focused on the sporty car. We had remained the unit directly behind the speeder and he had parked within a foot of the rear bumper. The other troopers moved in quickly.

To my surprise, and probably theirs, a young girl stepped from the driver's seat and promptly tumbled to the ground. She laughed and waved her arms about. "I surrender. Take me to your leader!" she shouted amid her giggles. It was hard to hear clearly with traffic whizzing by.

"Christ! She's wasted," one of the other troopers said.

Two of them moved to her sides and helped her stand. I got my first real good look at her. She was slender with an hourglass figure. Black hair cut in a ragged style, with bangs dangling in her eyes. She was wearing jeans, a short, tight leather jacket and a pair of leather boots that stopped just below her knee. The jacket was open. Judging by the size of her chest, I doubted if she could even zip it shut. The question of 'silicone or saline' jumped to mind.

"Who wants to party? I'll be the dancing girl!" She swayed to some unheard tune, rocking back and forth between the two cops.

Trooper Billings, the first officer on the scene, took charge. He brought out a portable Breathalyzer unit and administered the test. Legally drunk in this state is .08 percent. She blew .175 percent. Billings conferred with Kleinschmidt and one of the other officers before taking her by the arm.

"My dear, you have been driving under the influence of alcohol. I'm placing you under arrest," Billings said.

"Whazza big deal? Just let me go home, and I'll make you a happy cop!" She giggled at the sound of her own voice and slid an arm around his neck.

"Don't think my wife would appreciate that. C'mon, let's go for a nice little ride in the patrol car."

"What about my car? You can't just leave it here. That's my baby!" The girl cried as Billings snapped handcuffs around her wrists.

"A tow truck will haul your car to the impound yard. One of the guys will stay until the truck shows up to make sure nothing happens to it," Billings answered as he locked her in the back seat of the car. He turned and studied the faces of the other troopers. "Volunteers?"

"I'll wait," an older man named North answered.

"Thanks, Kenny. See you at the post. You'd better check her car for any other personal effects. "

"Looks like you got your hands full, Leo."

Billings glanced in the window at the girl who was struggling to open the door with her hands clasped behind her back. "No doubt," he said grimly. As Billings drove away, we could still see the girl in the back seat, squirming around. I wondered when reality would penetrate her intoxication. I also wondered if she had previous experience with handcuffs.

Kleinschmidt returned to his car and forced an opening in traffic by using his emergency lights. He didn't comment on my not following orders, but he didn't say anything else either. He drove to a family restaurant near the freeway and radioed for clearance to take a meal break. The place was decorated like a fifties style soda shop, with booths along the big glass window and a service counter with twenty vinyl covered stools. I expected the waitresses to wear saddle shoes and poodle skirts, but they opted for jeans, bobby sox, penny loafers and monogrammed blouses. Smitty was treated like a regular. After we ordered, he went to make a phone call. He came back quickly, and we discussed the girl who'd been arrested.

"According to what she told Billings, she's a dancer down at the Launch Pad. It's a strip club near the airport," Smitty explained.

I nodded. "I've heard of it. She seems too young to be dancing."

Kleinschmidt shrugged. "Nineteen. That's old enough to dance, but not old enough to drink. Claims she got off work at four and had one drink with her boss. There was a wad of cash in her purse and a pay stub from the place."

"What happens now?"

"She'll be tested again at the post. The level of intoxication will be reflected on the test. The more alcohol in her system, the longer she'll remain in custody. So much booze equals so many hours." He gave another shrug as the waitress brought our food.

I was working my way into a chicken salad when Smitty left to use the phone again. He came back shortly and proceeded to swallow half of his burger in two bites.

"Trouble?" I asked.

"I'm just hungry."

"I never would have guessed."

We didn't talk after that while we finished our meal. Kleinschmidt went to the phone twice more before we left. He was quiet. I was preoccupied, thinking about the events I'd witnessed so far. It was possible I had offended him somehow by not following his instructions about remaining with the car. I filled in my notes using the glare from the occasional passing headlights while the details were still fresh in my mind. It was a slow, silent ride into the darkness. Based on his mood, I expected the rest of the evening would be quiet.

We patrolled some of the surface streets for a while, delaying our return to the interstate. Kleinschmidt seemed restless. Maybe dinner hadn't agreed with him. If I bolted my meals that fast, my stomach would certainly revolt. We turned toward the approach ramp for the freeway and a pickup truck zoomed out of the dark, narrowly missing our front fender.

"What the hell was that?" Smitty snapped on the lights and the siren. The pickup was bathed in the red twirling light. The truck's color was a faded white, dotted along the fenders. Gradually it veered across the bridge for the interstate and eased over to the shoulder.

"Drunk driver?" I asked.

"It could be. Wait here." He glanced at me as he started to get out of the vehicle. "And I mean it this time."

"Okay, okay."

Smitty radioed in his location and climbed out of the patrol car. The spotlight mounted on his door was trained on the truck. Shadows filled the cab.

Kleinschmidt headed straight for the truck as the driver's door swung open. There was no one else on the road. No traffic of any kind. This section of the city didn't even have streetlights burning. This wasn't a residential area. It was more commercial, with little factories, probably the type that supported the auto industry. Around metropolitan Detroit, a majority of the businesses relate to the automotive industry in one form or another. Casually, I let my eyes drift over to the right, where the outline of a warehouse could just be seen beyond the cruiser's spotlight. I was wondering if Smitty would give this person a warning or if his indigestion would result in a ticket.

Suddenly, I saw a flash of light and heard a muffled bang. Smitty pitched onto his back, his right hand clawing feebly at his holster as a loud roar reached my ears. The door of the truck was still open, a brown arm extended beyond the edge of the spotlight. A gun was clutched in the gloved hand. I watched in horror as the trigger was pulled back for another shot.

Everything that happened next must have been instinct. Or maybe it was merely a reaction. Or dumb luck. Or the Force. Yeah, maybe it was the Force. I don't think I'll ever know for sure.

I reached across and pounded on the horn with one hand, flipping the buttons Smitty had used to activate the siren with the other. The sudden noise startled the driver. His arm jerked back into the cab and the door slammed. Spraying stones and dust behind, the truck lurched onto the road and raced away.

Fumbling the microphone off the dash, I thumbed the button. "Kleinschmidt has been shot! Send an ambulance!" I dropped the microphone and managed to get my door open. The frame around the window clipped my forehead and knocked me back a step.

I'd forgotten to turn off the siren and its wail was splitting my eardrums. "Idiot," I muttered, "stay calm." This was easier to say than it ever was to do.

Reaching back inside, I switched the siren off then rushed around to the front of the car. Smitty was lying on his back on the edge of the road. Blood soaked the gravel beneath him. His eyes were closed, but I could see his chest moving.

I dropped to my knees beside him. "You're going to be okay, Smitty. I called for help."

"Shot by a dog," he whispered. Kleinschmidt opened his eyes weakly. "First aid kit in the trunk. Stop the bleeding." His voice was fading so fast I had to press my ear above his mouth. I got a whiff of grilled onions.

What if the truck came back? What if they were waiting

right now, just beyond the reach of the spotlight, waiting for me to get close so they could kill Smitty? And kill the witness too? I cringed. They wouldn't need to shoot us, just drive right over us with that truck. My imagination was running away with possibilities.

With a shake of my head, I chased such thoughts away. I ran back to the car. I dropped the keys three times after getting them out of the ignition before finally jamming the right one into the trunk lock. There was a white metal box with a red cross on it. I lugged it back to Smitty and knelt beside him. Where the hell was that ambulance?

There were latex gloves inside the kit on top of all the equipment. I pulled them on and rummaged through the contents. I found some large sterile gauze pads and some medical tape. Somehow I managed to crudely tape the gauze to each side of his shoulder. The bullet had entered through a small hole just beneath the collarbone on his right side. The exit wound looked bigger than a golf ball.

"You're going to be all right, Smitty." I don't know if I said this for his benefit or mine.

He groaned and closed his eyes again.

I didn't know what else to do. I'd called for help. I'd patched him up. There was no way I could move him. But I didn't think I was supposed to anyway. I thought he was still breathing, but I wasn't sure. Closed eyes meant death. I was sure of it.

I rocked forward and slapped his cheek. Hard. "Don't you die on me!" I screamed.

His eyes fluttered open.

My limited medical knowledge flashed through my mind—coma, shock, heart attack, trauma, tonsillitis. I had no idea what else to do for him. Where were the professionals? They should have been here already!

My eyes kept flicking from Smitty's face, to his wound, to the direction the truck had taken. Suddenly I heard the sound of a siren. Then another joined in. I swiveled my head, trying to find them. Another groan escaped Smitty's lips. My eyes searched his body for signs of life. I thought it was too late.

The siren sounded close now. I glanced up as the ambulance and another patrol car arrived.

"What the hell took you guys so long?" I shouted as they rushed to us. The paramedics rudely pushed me aside and bent over Smitty. I was about to kick one guy squarely in the ass when someone grabbed me from behind and lifted me off the ground. I was carried back to Smitty's car, struggling all the way. Finally, they sat me down on the hood. My eyes focused and I recognized Sergeant Malone.

"Relax, Jamie. Let the paramedics do their job."

I was exasperated. How could he be so calm when one of his own men lay there wounded? "He could be dead by now, Malone. He's been lying there bleeding for over an hour."

"It hasn't been an hour. It's only been three minutes." Malone tried to smile but it never reached his eyes.

"Three minutes?"

"Three minutes. Your call came in two minutes after Smitty radioed in his position. His report was logged in at ten-fourteen. Your call was at ten-sixteen. It's now ten-nineteen."

"Three minutes?" I repeated.

"That's all, Jamie." Malone pointed over my shoulder to the ambulance. They were already loading Smitty into the back of the wagon. One of the medics waved at Malone, flashing a thumbs up signal. Malone returned the gesture.

"He's okay?"

"He's not going to die. Kleinschmidt's damn lucky you were riding with him tonight. Help might not have gotten here so quickly if it weren't for you." We watched the ambulance race away, sirens wailing. The hospital was two miles up the road.

"It all happened so fast."

After giving me a few more minutes to calm down, Malone got behind the wheel of Smitty's car and drove us to the hospital. Trooper North had brought him from the station and rushed to the scene. Several times during the ride, he asked me to go over the details of the shooting.

"It was an old pickup truck, maybe a Ford. Kleinschmidt pulled it over when the truck almost hit us, as we were about to enter the freeway. The pickup didn't have any lights on. I remember the cab was dark, even when Smitty turned the spotlight on it. I couldn't see inside."

"Don't suppose you caught the license number?" Malone asked.

"CJ 1134."

He looked surprised. "You're sure about that?"

"Positive. I wrote it down in my notebook when Kleinschmidt pulled it over. I'd been making notes all night long." Even now I clutched a pen in one hand, my book in the other.

Malone called the station with the information. The dispatcher would relay it on the air, alerting the other units to search for it. Approach with caution, suspect wanted in the assault on Trooper Kleinschmidt.

At the hospital, we talked to the emergency room physician. Smitty was stable going into surgery. The doctor suspected a number of tears to the blood vessels and ligaments in his shoulder. Unlike the movies, it was going to take a lot more than two aspirin and a Sesame Street bandage to put Kleinschmidt back together again.

Bert Nowalski arrived a few minutes later and pulled Malone over for a briefing. Then Bert approached me. There was no friendly smile this time.

"Malone will escort you back to your vehicle, Jamie. You did a great job calling it in when Kleinschmidt got hit. Now go home."

"I'd rather wait and make sure Smitty's okay."

"That won't be necessary. Sergeant Malone will cover the rest of Trooper Kleinschmidt's patrol. I'll remain here, to confer with the doctors when he comes out of surgery.

He won't be allowed visitors right away."

"Then let me finish the shift with Malone." I didn't like being dismissed so easily.

Bert ignored me. "We had a deal. Take her back to the station, Malone. I think you've had enough excitement for one night, Jamie."

My temper was rising. "It's not fair. If I hadn't..."

"C'mon, Jamie," Malone said as he lightly tugged at my arm. "There's nothing else you can do here."

I put the heels of my hands against my forehead and pressed hard. It was a trick my mother had taught me to control my temper. Sometimes it worked, but not tonight. I forced out a breath. "What the hell! Take me back to my car, Malone."

* * * *

Saturday, I called the hospital as soon as I awoke. Kleinschmidt was resting comfortably and out of danger. The doctors didn't know yet if he'd regain full use of his arm. I picked up some candy (he didn't strike me as the type of guy who'd like flowers) and a few hunting magazines and went to visit him. Several off-duty cops were hanging around his bed when I poked my head in the door. Malone was among them.

"Hi, Jamie, thanks for coming by," Smitty said.

"No problem." I handed over the goodies and glanced at his wound. His shoulder was heavily taped and his right arm was in a sling across his chest.

"What some guys won't do to get out of a Saturday night patrol," Malone joked.

The cops bantered back and forth, exchanging remarks about last night. "Tell Kleinschmidt what happened, Sarge," Kenny North urged.

Malone glanced at me then began the story. "When Billings brought in Nicole, she was still flying. She blew .165 percent on the scale. It was going to be at least eight hours before she came back to earth. Robin was downstairs, helping the dispatcher."

"Robin's a female trooper," Billings said for my benefit.

"Anyway, Robin comes in to pat her down. While Nicole is up against the wall, she closes her eyes and starts doing her routine."

"No way!" Smitty said.

"Way. All she's got on is the jacket, jeans and boots and one of those camisoles under the jacket. Robin turns her around and the kid keeps on dancing."

"Tell them what Robin did," North said.

"She goes about her business. Robin checks the girl's arms, legs and pockets for a weapon. Nicole drops her jacket and thrusts her breasts at Robin."

I was caught up in the image of the young dancer, drunkenly performing. "What did she do?"

"Nicole asks Robin if she likes her breasts," Malone, obviously an experienced storyteller, paused making certain he had everyone's attention. "Rob says, 'Nah, I've got better. And mine are real.' Shut the kid right up."

Billings picked up the story. "We put her in holding for a few minutes while I process the paperwork. She's cuffed to the wall. Routine is to transfer her to a city jail if she has to be in for more than a few hours. While I'm finishing up, Rothman puts a guy in with her. When I get ready to run her over to Livonia's, she's trying to get the guy to pay her to dance. She said she still has to make payments on her enhancements."

"Told you those weren't real," North said.

Old stories about high-speed chases and strange arrests followed. I got the feeling these were more for my benefit than Kleinschmidt's. He'd probably heard them many times before.

The conversation eventually touched on the governor's plan. I watched Smitty's eyes when someone mentioned the pending cutbacks for the troopers.

"Tough break, Smitty. Looks like you're going to be on

the wrong side of Axman's list when it rolls through next month," Leo Billings said.

"Guess you and me will be hitting the unemployment line with the greenies," another trooper chuckled.

"Forget it, Madison. I don't take charity," Smitty said sternly.

"You won't have much to worry about," Malone said, "you'll be drawing regular pay until that shoulder wound heals."

A young Hispanic nurse came in to give Kleinschmidt a shot and shooed us all out. Malone pulled me aside as the rest of the cops headed out to the parking lot.

"Herman backed up your version about the truck, even down to the license number."

"Herman?"

He smiled. "Now you know why he goes by Smitty. But he never got a good look at the driver. Did you?"

"No. All I saw was an arm sticking out of the cab. Have you found the truck?"

Malone shook his head. "The plates are registered to a guy in Milford. Turns out he reported them stolen, about two weeks ago. And they belonged to his Chevy van, not a pickup truck."

"So what do you do now?"

"Keep digging. If whoever shot Smitty doesn't dump the truck, it might still have the plates on it. We could find prints inside, too. The captain sent a crime scene team out last night. They found the slug stuck in a road sign. They also checked the area for tire treads. We may be able to match the treads with a specific pattern, and trace the vehicle that way."

"Is it permissible to say this case doesn't sound very promising?" I didn't want him to leave yet.

"Let's just say I've seen better odds. Something will turn up." He guided me to a waiting room with a vending machine, some of those uncomfortable plastic formed chairs and a television set bolted to the wall. Saturday morning cartoon characters ran around zapping each other with lasers. Good clean fun. No one ever gets seriously injured in the cartoon world. "Buy you a coffee?"

"Sure."

We were the only ones in the room. I found the button and silenced the cartoons. We sat by the window, sipping the scalding bitter brew. If there is anything worse than vending machine coffee, I haven't found it yet.

"Hope this doesn't ruin your idea for a story," Malone said.

"Not at all. It was very informative, even before the shooting."

"I get the feeling Nowalski wouldn't jump to let you observe again, no matter who you know."

I wondered if Malone knew of my relationship with Bert. Probably not. Bert always said he kept his personal life personal and his professional life professional. I shrugged and did my best to keep the conversation going. "Can't say I blame him. But I wish he had let me finish the shift with you last night. Or at least hang out at the hospital."

Malone shrugged. "Wasn't much to see. By the time I dropped you off, it was almost time for Kleinschmidt's tour to end. All I did was park his unit and file the reports. You didn't miss anything, Jamie. All the action was over by that point."

I batted my lashes at him. "I didn't even get to see the locker room."

"Some things are better left to your imagination." Malone finished his coffee and crumpled the cardboard cup. With a flick of his wrist he sent it across the room and into a small garbage can. Two points.

"I have a very vivid imagination, Malone." I imitated his shot. My cup went soaring out into the hallway.

Malone's eyes had drifted from my face for a moment. I realized his gaze was smoothly moving down my body. "I'll bet you do."

35

I blushed. Where had my sassy comment come from? Twelve hours after witnessing a shooting, I'm flirting up a storm. I looked away from Malone and made a show of digging in my purse for my keys. He watched me without comment, his eyes on my face now. Malone seemed to be enjoying my discomfort.

He walked me out to my car and held the door for me as I wiggled inside.

"Feel free to call me if you have any questions, Jamie."

"I might just do that. Will you let me know if you learn anything about Smitty's assailant?"

He gave me that soft smile. One of my butterflies came back to tickle my stomach. Or maybe it was the coffee. "Sure."

"Good luck, Malone."

"Thanks, Jamie."

CHAPTER FOUR

I talked to Bert on Sunday. Since the whole gang had been to see him, Smitty was now pulling a Marlene Dietrich. He wanted to be left alone. Bert thanked me twice for my efforts Friday night.

"If you need any details for the story you're working on, just call me. It may be hard for you to believe, but I used to do uniform patrols too."

I tried to downplay the concern evident in his voice. "Wow. Did they have cars back then, or did you patrol in a horse and buggy?"

"Don't be a wise ass, little girl. Your mother didn't raise you to be so sarcastic."

"Where do you think I learned it?"

He snorted laughter over the line. "You have a point."

"Don't worry about me, Bert. But keep me informed about Kleinschmidt. I'd really like to know how he's doing."

"I'll call you if there's any change. But don't beat yourself up on this, Jamie. It would have happened no matter what. Kleinschmidt's lucky you were there."

I wondered if I would ever be able to put the shooting out of my mind that easily.

* * * *

For three days I couldn't write a damn thing. No matter how hard I tried to concentrate, all I could think about was Kleinschmidt, leaping backwards in the glow of the headlights as the gun went off. I'd never seen anyone shot before. It's not the same as in the movies, where you know the guy is going to get up and walk away when the cameras stop rolling. This was for keeps. And it scared the hell out of me.

It turned out Smitty wasn't as lucky as the doctors originally thought. When the bullet entered, it began to tumble and turn, causing a lot of nerve damage. Unless physical therapy was extremely successful, Kleinschmidt might never recover full use of his arm. Even additional surgery might not restore the arm to full working order. Ironically, with the governor's cutbacks scheduled to start in January, Smitty's career with the state law enforcement could very easily have ended anyway.

I visited him a couple of times at the hospital, but he refused to talk to me. The nurses said he was trying to stay positive about his situation, but it wasn't easy. As a joke I sent him a box of donuts, hoping to ease the tension. No luck. Apparently Smitty couldn't find anything funny right now. I went for a drive and realized I'd been circling the state police post. Maybe someone here would be willing to talk to me about Kleinschmidt.

Malone was in the lobby when I walked inside. He offered me that glimmer of a warm smile as I approached.

"How are you doing, Jamie?" Once again I was surprised at the melodious softness of his voice.

"Okay, Malone. Is there anything new on Kleinschmidt's shooter?"

He shook his head once. "Forensics came up empty. The little bit of tire tread they were able to lift from the scene is too worn to make a match. We found no shell casing at the time of the shooting, but Smitty said the gun was a revolver, maybe a .38 caliber."

"Didn't you find the slug?" I asked as he led me to the coffee machine.

"Yeah, but there's nothing we can do with it until we find a gun to run comparisons. Either that, or another bullet to match it with." Malone grimaced as he sipped the vending machine coffee.

"What about the truck?"

"Nothing's turned up. It's almost as if the thing disappeared into thin air." Malone made a face and dumped the remainder of his coffee down the drain. "Waste of money."

I fought the urge to smile. "What's going to happen to Smitty? The doctors won't tell me anything in detail"

"Because he was injured in the line of duty, he'll receive his regular pay until he recovers. If he never regains full use of the arm, he wouldn't be able to pass the physical. In which case, he'll be medically retired and receive two thirds of his pay, tax free, for life. Financially, Smitty's got nothing to worry about." Malone guided me back to the private office and closed the door behind us. "I understand he won't talk to you."

"I've been to the hospital a couple of times. What's he got against me?" I took the extra chair and slumped into it, crossing my ankles before me.

"Maybe he's embarrassed. Quick thinking on your part may have saved his life. There isn't a hell of a lot of traffic on that stretch of road at night." Malone leaned against the edge of his desk

"So why won't he talk to me?"

"Maybe he just wants to be left alone. As far as I know, the only one he'll see is his girlfriend."

I was surprised. "He won't talk to you either?"

Malone shook his head. I studied the cool shade of his blue eyes, reminding me again of cobalt. I wondered what happened to the humor I'd seen when we'd first met. It hadn't been visible since. Maybe I'd imagined it. But there was something else now, hiding in the corners. It felt like he had x-ray vision. He didn't need to undress me with his eyes. He could see right through me.

"Kleinschmidt isn't talking to anyone else. Even Captain Nowalski gets nothing more than grunts." He checked the clock and pushed off the desk. "Sorry to cut this short, Jamie, but I've got roll call in thirty seconds. If I learn anything else, I'll let you know."

"Thanks, Malone." He held the door for me as I went down the hall toward the main entrance. When I glanced back, he was standing there, watching me. I waved. He waved back. I haven't waved at a guy since high school. Was he flirting with me? I could only hope.

* * * *

One week after the shooting I was still in a rut. Work was impossible. No matter how long I sat before the keyboard, nothing flowed from my fingers. After an hour each morning, I gave up and puttered around the apartment. The plants got watered, the laundry not only done but neatly folded and put away. When it came down to cleaning the oven, I knew I'd crossed the line. A lunch date with Bert was pretty much the first time I left the house in a while.

He took me to Rocky's, a great little tavern not far from the post. The owner had previously been a top chef with a local chain of upscale seafood restaurants. He liked to experiment with unusual combinations. The special on Friday was lobster ravioli in a light cream sauce. It was accompanied by a mixed green salad including dried cherries and pecans. A small loaf of freshly baked cheesy garlic bread completed the feast. We both had the special and could hardly move after the meal.

"You eat this well all the time?" I asked.

"Hell no. I haven't been here a dozen times in five

years. But how often do I get to sneak away for lunch with a lovely young woman?"

"You feed me like this I'll visit you for a meal every day."

Bert sipped his coffee and nodded. "Yeah, and within two weeks, you'd be running for the border. Don't kid yourself, Jamie Rae. You like that independence."

I felt my cheeks flush. "What do you mean?"

"You know perfectly well what I mean. Since I've known you, it's been only a matter of minutes before you wanted to be on your own. You've got a touch of your mother's free spirit. That's why you preferred freelancing. You can change your directions at a whim. There is nothing to tie you down."

Silently, I considered his observation. I did like being on my own. There were no pets at the apartment, just a few plants for atmosphere. More often than not, two weeks went by before I remembered to water them.

"You think I really prefer being on my own?"

Bert gave me a muscular shrug. "Hey, there's nothing wrong with it. I'm sure you've had your share of romantic relationships. Maybe someday, you'll find a guy you can tolerate who can tolerate you."

"You're starting to sound like a social worker with a twenty-two-inch neck."

"I don't get the chance to talk to you that often. I know it's not easy to hear, but you might benefit from seeing things from my perspective."

I lowered my gaze to the coffee cup. "Shut up, Bert."

"Now there's the Jamie I know and love. But don't think I'm some kind of expert. The longest relationship I had was with your mother. That should tell you something."

I didn't comment while he paid the bill. Only as we were gathering our coats did I zing him back.

"I think what that tells me is that you're a hopeless romantic. You fell in love one time with Vera and even though you've been divorced all these years, you still have feelings for her." I linked my arm with his.

"Now who's the social worker?"

"You still love her."

It was his turn. "Shut up, Jamie," he said with a playful smile on his face.

Bert walked me to my car. The wind was gusting, yanking the last remaining leaves from the trees. The temperature had dropped dramatically. Soon winter would be upon us. I leaned against Bert, stretching up to kiss his cheek. "I'll take that as a yes."

"After high school and those teenage crushes, I've only loved three women my whole life. Not a lot, but enough for me. One was Elaine, my first wife."

I nodded with the memory. Bert kept a small portrait of her on his dresser, even when he'd been married to Vera. Elaine had died from an aneurysm. No warning at all. She was twenty-seven. One moment, she was walking down the aisle of the grocery store. The next, she was dead. "She was lovely. I remember her picture."

He opened my door and waved me inside. "Still hurts sometimes, just thinking about her. Then there was Vera. And we all know where that went."

Bert ducked his head inside my car and planted a kiss on my cheek. "Be good, Jamie." He pulled away and firmly closed my door.

He was almost to his car when I realized what he'd said. I drove across the parking lot and lowered my window. "You said three. Who else?"

"That's you, Jamie Rae."

Sometimes, I can be so dense.

* * * *

I turned down a dinner invitation from my aunt and theater tickets from an old girlfriend. I still couldn't focus on my work for more than an hour at a time. Friday night at ten-fourteen, I went back to the scene. I sat in my Honda and stared at the space where my life came apart. Why was I so upset? Smitty didn't die. The bad guy had split when I hit the siren. Maybe he'd never be whole again, but it's better than being dead. That should count for something. At least, I thought so.

Without the engine running, the cold crept into my car. Winter was coming. I closed my eyes and saw the shooting again. It happened in vivid slow motion, with Kleinschmidt moving toward the truck then floating backward like a gymnast on a tumbling mat. Blinking, I swore the gun roared again as my eyes adjusted to the darkness. There was nothing out there, just an instant replay on the theater screen in my mind, complete with surround sound and dazzling special effects.

Who would do such a thing? Nobody could have known Smitty would be patrolling this area after dinner. He had mentioned earlier that he seldom ate at the same place two nights in a row. Variety helped break the monotony of any job. Work wouldn't be a problem for him anymore. I wondered what kind of routine he might become accustomed to now. Would he survive as a one-armed man?

Kleinschmidt just happened to be in the wrong place at the wrong time. What would have happened if Smitty hadn't stopped the truck? What if we'd gone for pizza? What if he'd taken an earlier dinner break?

After a while I drove away from the scene and cruised. I went west in the same direction the truck had taken, away from the interstate and the city. A couple of curves around a grove of trees and I was on a gravel road I didn't know existed. This was part of the industrial complex Malone had mentioned. Factories lined the right side, backing up to the interstate. A self-storage facility was on the left, next to a huge auto parts yard. Old cars were stacked ten high, reaching into the dark night, like shaky offerings to a prehistoric god. I turned around and drove home. Something crept across the back of my mind but I couldn't quite grasp it. I stopped by the factories and stared at the surroundings for a few minutes. Nothing was clicking. Frustrated, I gave up and headed for home.

Cops put their lives on the line every day they put on their uniforms. Maybe they're fearless, or ready to die. Maybe it's part of their training, to be ready for such situations. Maybe there's a psychological test they have to take, before going to the academy, to make sure they can deal with situations like this. Even though I'd known what Bert had done for years, I was developing a new respect for him and all the other cops I knew even casually from my time as a reporter. They are a tough breed. I was only a witness to a shooting. It hadn't even been a fatal shooting, but it was enough to haunt me. I was beginning to wonder if it would haunt me the rest of my life.

Early Saturday morning, I awoke with a start and couldn't fall back to sleep. I waited until dawn broke, then dressed and retraced my route.

I managed to drive past the scene of the shooting without shaking, an improvement over yesterday. My brain kept trying to point something out, but I was too groggy to see it. I rounded the second curve, past the grove of trees. The road splits there. The right fork takes you to the industrial area, the left swings back to the south, circling toward the freeway. I went to the right.

Despite the early hour, the auto parts yard was open for business. As I parked beside the gate, the meanest dog I've ever seen greeted me. It was one part Doberman, one part German shepherd, ten parts ugly. In case the dog was as smart as he was ugly, I locked my door and stayed inside.

A shrill whistle broke the morning air and the dog quickly retreated to a pen near the office building. A burly man wearing farmer's overalls and a purple tee shirt dropped a bowl of food inside the cage for the dog, then swung the gate shut on the pen. I stepped out of the car as

44

he approached. I hoped he was friendlier than his four-legged friend.

"Morning, Miss. Hope Brutus didn't startle you," he said as he drew alongside.

"Just caught me off guard. Are you the owner?"

He grinned widely, revealing a row of tobacco-stained teeth. "That'd be the bank. I just run the place. Name's Joe Garibaldi. What can I do for you?"

"I was looking for a pickup truck. My uncle owns one, and it's falling apart. I wondered if you had anything for sale."

Joe grinned again and swept his arms wide. "Everything's for sale. But I can't guarantee anything here's in better shape than what your uncle's already got."

I followed his gesture and took a closer look at the cars. Most of them were missing fenders or hoods. Some were mere shells, even the upholstery, doors and windows gone.

"This is more of a graveyard than a used car lot. People bring their wrecks in, and we strip `em down for working parts. When we get down to the bare bones, we crush `em and sell the scrap steel." Garibaldi led me a few steps farther into the yard. "What kind of truck does your uncle have? Maybe we can fix him up with the parts he needs to keep it running."

"That would be cheaper than buying a new one," I said thoughtfully. "Does it make any difference between model years?"

"Nah, not if you're close. Trucks don't usually change much from year to year. Find out what he's got, and the kind of stuff he needs. We're bound to be able to help him out."

"Thanks, Joe." We had wandered over to the dog's cage. He was curled next to the empty bowl, sleeping peacefully. "So long, Brutus."

"He'll sleep like the dead, `til closing time. Nobody gets past Brutus."

"I'll take your word for it."

Garibaldi walked away as a wrecker pulled into the yard with a badly damaged Plymouth van. I slipped back into the Honda and drove away.

I stopped at a diner for a breakfast that would make a cardiologist cringe. After consuming a sausage, mushroom and Swiss cheese omelet, toast with jam and hash browns, I felt considerably better. Once home, I sacked out on the couch and took a long nap. It was early afternoon when the phone woke me. I tried to sound healthy and coherent, but the receiver was upside down in my hand.

"'lo."

"Hi, Jamie. Got a minute?"

"Whozzit?"

"Malone. Did I wake you up?"

I shuddered and rubbed my face with both hands, squeezing the phone against my ear. "Yeah, I must have dozed off. What's up?"

"I was wondering if you're free this evening. Maybe take in dinner and a movie, or something." His mellow voice was hypnotic.

"Thought you worked nights," I mumbled.

"It's my weekend off. I get one every three weeks. What do you say? I know this is short notice and all, but..."

I wasn't letting him off that easy. "Sure, Malone. What time's good?"

"Six-thirty. I'll pick you up. See you later."

"See ya."

* * * *

Malone was punctual. Normally I'm always early, because I don't like to rush. If I have a business meeting, I pick out the outfit I'm going to wear the night before. Otherwise it makes me uncomfortable. Tonight, I must have changed clothes ten times, trying to pick out a suitable outfit. What does one wear when dating a cop?

Leather and handcuffs? Mirrored sunglasses? A battered fedora with a trench coat? I settled on a denim skirt and a thick cotton sweater in a soft lavender shade. Underneath was a matching lavender ensemble. Tan pantyhose and comfortable black pumps with two-inch heels. I'd picked out one thin gold necklace and small dangling earrings. Malone was wearing a sport shirt and slacks, with a pair of boots and a leather jacket.

"Hi, Malone."

"Hi, Jamie. Hey, you've got legs," he said with a smile. The combined effect of his smile and killer voice weakened my knees.

"Some say they're my best feature."

"They're nice, but I don't know if they're your best."

I blushed. Now I wondered what he was referring to. "Come on in. Is there anything new on Kleinschmidt?"

Malone nodded as he sat on the sofa. I tried to hide my grin as the cushions swallowed him up. "He started physical therapy last Monday. Captain Nowalski talked to him this morning. Kleinschmidt says he wants to concentrate completely on his rehabilitation."

"That sounds antisocial to me. Was Kleinschmidt ever a hermit?" I opted for the bentwood rocker. The sofa has a tendency to push two occupants together, like a persistent Jewish aunt.

"Smitty's just a private guy. He never hung out with the others at the post, didn't show up for the poker games or the bachelor parties. Kind of a loner."

"That reminds me of a caveman's attitude." I thumped my chest with a forefinger. "Big man take care of self. No need others."

"You always make fun of cops?"

"Only when I'm nervous. And it's not just cops. At times, I make fun of everybody. I'm just having a hard time understanding Smitty. If the situation was reversed, I'd expect everyone I've ever met to come visit me."

"People deal with problems differently." He shifted on

the cushions. I wondered if he was going to disappear.

"You want a drink, or some coffee?"

"I'm fine."

"So what's up for this evening?" I realized my legs had crossed on their own accord. From Malone's position on the sofa, he could see right up my skirt if he wanted to. But his eyes were on my face. Maybe not all men are sleaze.

"Care for Italian food?"

"Are you kidding?" I rolled my eyes in delight. "I'm a sucker for calamari, antipasto salad, veal piccata, pasta primavera, eggplant parmesan. Did you have a particular place in mind?"

"Dominic's?"

"That sounds great. It's bound to be crowded."

He smiled, all the way to the eyes. "I made reservations. Ready?"

"You're pretty sure of yourself, Malone." I held back a giggle as he struggled out of the clutches of the sofa.

"Not really. I made reservations at three restaurants, Italian, Japanese and vegetarian." He helped me on with my wool coat.

"Vegetarian? A cop who's a vegetarian?"

"Not me. But I'm always open to new experiences. After hearing you recite the menu, I realized how long it's been since I've had good Italian food."

I linked my arm in his. "You've got me salivating, Malone. Let's go."

CHAPTER FIVE

I have to admit to being more than a little apprehensive about the evening. First dates are always a pain in the ass. Those damn butterflies in my stomach were running rampant. It had been a while since I'd been out with someone new.

If Malone noticed my shaky state, he was too much of a gentleman to mention it. A couple of glasses of Chianti helped calm me down during dinner. The food was exceptional. From the appetizer of mussels marinara through the veal (parmesan for me, piccata for Malone), we ate continuously for an hour and a half. When we left the restaurant, my butterflies were gone. Probably crushed by the amount of food I'd consumed, or choking in a dozen cloves of garlic.

After dinner we went to a small jazz club Malone knew and danced for several hours. Time was a blur. He was light on his feet and good company, maintaining his end of the conversation with humorous stories. The first couple of dances were easy and smooth. The more we danced, the closer he held me. My body was picking up on signals that my brain tried desperately to ignore. There was no denying how much I was enjoying myself. The evening ended too soon.

We were back at my place, waiting for coffee to brew. Malone slid onto the sofa, and disappeared from view. I set the tray with the mugs, cream and sugar on the table before us and made the mistake of sitting beside him.

"Hey," I said softly, as the sofa pressed us together.

"People could vanish in a thing like this." His arm automatically went around me.

"Amelia Earhart had one. So did Elvis."

"Jimmy Hoffa probably did, too." Our lips met tenderly, the sofa working its magic. My face felt flushed as Malone's hand stroked my cheek.

"I should warn you. This couch was a present from my mother. She's still hoping for grandchildren." My voice sounded funny and my breath was catching in my throat.

"Kids could use this as a trampoline." Malone's breath tickled my ear as he spoke.

It was hopeless to resist but I tried one last time. "Coffee should be ready. How do you take it?"

Malone leaned back just far enough to look in my eyes. I wanted to go swimming in those icy blue orbs. "Black."

He must have seen the grimace cross my face. "I have to warn you; I make really bad coffee."

"As bad as vending machines?"

"Depending on your taste buds, maybe worse."

There was just the briefest moment of hesitation. "I'll take my chances."

It was a struggle to push him deeper into the sofa and climb out. I don't know which was more difficult, getting away from the clutches of the cushions or fighting my impulse to jump him. My whole body was flushed. I knew it wasn't that warm in the apartment. I managed to get into the kitchen and retrieve the pot. When I came back, Malone had moved to the rocker.

"You okay?"

He nodded. "Things started moving a little too fast."

It was my turn to nod. Not trusting myself to speak, I

poured him a mug of coffee then fiddled with one for me. I knew better than to sit on the sofa, so I perched on the edge of the table.

Malone was brave, sensible and fearless.

He drank the coffee. Then winked at me.

"Worse than vending machines?" I asked.

"No," he said quietly, "but it could be a close race."

I sipped mine. There was enough sugar and cream in it to make a milkshake. I shuddered at the thought of drinking it black.

"Think I'd better be going," Malone said. He rose effortlessly out of the rocker and hooked my wrist with his fingers. I moved closer for a kiss. He met me halfway.

"You could stay," I whispered.

"Not this time."

"I wouldn't mind."

The smile reached all the way to his eyes. "I'm old-fashioned."

"Will I see you again?" It was every girl's anxious question.

He kissed me lightly on the mouth then kissed both my eyelids. I was melting. "Free tomorrow?"

"You mean Sunday tomorrow or Monday tomorrow?" I kept my eyes closed. If I opened them too soon, he'd be gone and I might have imagined the whole evening.

"Sunday tomorrow, for brunch?"

"It's a date."

* * * *

Soaking in a huge bubble bath, filled with fragrant, tropical oils, I had just been pampered with a massage, facial, manicure and pedicure. My hair was shampooed and styled. In the distance, I could see Malone, anxiously waiting for me. Beyond him was an elaborate buffet filled with delicacies. Slowly, I became aware of the welcoming aroma of rich gourmet coffee. I swam up from the depths of the dream, realizing the coffee smell was real.

Blinking at the clock, I saw it was nine-thirty. It was almost three when Malone left. Had I left the coffee pot on all night?

Rolling out of bed, I yanked open the bedroom door and froze in place. Malone was sitting at the counter by the kitchen. In front of him was the enormous Sunday paper. On the counter was a mug of coffee. I could see the steam rising from it. Before he could turn I jumped back behind the door and shut it with a slam.

"Malone! What are you doing here?"

There was no immediate response while he walked over. "Morning, Jamie. We had a brunch date."

"Yeah, brunch. That is the combination of breakfast and lunch. The sun's barely up," I said with a growl. I didn't dare look at myself in the mirror. I needed a shower, shampoo and makeup before I'd be willing to even look myself in the eye, let alone a guy. Men! Are they absolutely clueless about what a woman goes through each and every morning?

"Hey, I can come back later."

I hesitated. If I let him go, would he really come back?

"Jamie?"

"Malone, I need some time to get ready. You know, girl time. Not the five minutes it takes a guy to shower, pull on jeans and walk out the door."

From the other side of the door, I could hear him chuckle. "How much time?"

I almost fell for it. If I said thirty minutes and it took me an hour, I'd never forgive myself. If I said an hour and it took more, I'd probably never see Malone again.

"Jamie, I could leave and come back," he said again.

The words blurted out of my mouth with no connection to my brain. "Stay put, Malone. Go drink your coffee and read the paper. But do not cast your eyes in my direction until I say so. Deal?"

Now he was laughing in earnest. "Deal. Do you trust

me, Jamie?"

I took a moment to consider it. "Mostly."

"That's a start."

I listened to him walk away. Then I dug a hooded robe out of the closet I seldom wear and covered every visible inch of me. After peeking out the door and making sure he was at the counter, I raced for the bathroom.

Men!

Sixty minutes later I'd showered, shampooed, flossed and brushed my teeth. A quick application of makeup and perfume and I was almost ready. I curled my hair, which takes some time to get the right look. I'm not one of those beauties who can roll out of bed, give her head a quick shake and have everything fall into place.

Now I simply had to travel the distance between the bath and my bedroom. Then it was a matter of picking out the right clothes. Throwing the robe over my shoulders, I yanked open the door and stepped into the hall.

And froze.

Malone calmly stood between the bedroom door and me. The rat!

He was fighting valiantly to keep the smile off his face. But his eyes were giving him away. I watched him struggle to keep his expression calm and his attention on my face. I spun around, pulling the robe around me to cover what he'd already seen.

"Hey, Jamie. I was just bringing you some coffee." His voice was steady, but I could sense the laughter welling up inside him.

"A likely story, Malone. I told you no peeking."

I brushed past him and darted into my bedroom. As I was closing the door, I saw his hand press against the wood, halting its progress. His other hand moved slowly through the opening. Without another word, he passed me one of my ceramic mugs. It was filled with hot coffee. Silently, I took it from him. He withdrew his hand and pulled the door shut.

I sipped it. He'd even mixed in cream and sugar, just as I liked it. But this couldn't have come from my coffee pot. This was good. I gulped half of it down then shed the robe.

Ten minutes later, I was dressed in jeans and a red turtleneck sweater. Malone neatly folded the paper on the counter and eased off the stool.

"How did you get in?"

He shrugged. "I knocked, but there was no answer. You didn't lock your door."

"It's a quiet neighborhood and a really safe apartment building. I hardly ever lock the door."

He leaned over and gave me a tender kiss. "Ready to go?"

"Sure. But I don't know how much I'll eat. I'm still stuffed from dinner."

"We'll see."

Malone wouldn't say where we were going. He drove west, headed toward Ann Arbor. We passed the city and kept going. An hour later, we were outside of Jackson. He turned off the highway and began zigging and zagging through two lane roads. We ended up at a country inn. A small lake was in the background. A string quartet was playing softly. Buffet tables laden with everything from fresh fruit to venison lined one wall. At the end was a chef in the traditional whites with a Red Wings baseball cap on his gray head. He was making omelets big enough to feed a family of four.

"Hungry?" Malone asked quietly as I stood there surveying the bounty before me. I noticed the dining room was packed and many people were waiting in the lobby.

"Suddenly, I'm starved."

He steered me back to the hostess stand. There was a frazzled young woman standing at the podium. She smiled valiantly as we approached.

"Happy Sunday. Do you have reservations for the buffet?" Her voice was as squeaky as a cartoon character.

I was shaking my head no when Malone indicated that we did. She scrolled down the list, made a checkmark against his name and led us to a table overlooking the lake.

We started with coffee, giving the crowd at the buffet line a chance to thin out.

"That's pretty impressive that you made reservations and got me here on time, Malone."

His eyes twinkled over the rim of his coffee cup. "A very wise man once said, timing is everything."

"I'm betting you didn't make the reservations this morning," I said.

"Nope, I made them yesterday."

"You're pretty sure of yourself, Sergeant."

"It goes with the territory."

Brunch was a long, leisurely meal that seemed to last three hours. We went slowly through the buffet line, sampling the delicacies. There was smoked salmon, pate, venison tenderloin with mushrooms and capers in a brandy cream sauce, deviled eggs, roasted potatoes with garlic and chives. And that was just on the first plate.

After brunch we walked along the lake, enjoying the crisp autumn air. It wouldn't be much longer before the snow began to fly. Already, the days were noticeably shorter.

On the drive home, Malone stayed on the state roads, rather than hit the freeway. It was almost as if he didn't want the day to end. I know I certainly didn't. Somewhere along the drive back, he'd taken my hand and held it gently. For stretches at a time, we were silent. Then a song on the stereo would trigger a comment, and we'd chatter away like old friends.

We walked slowly up the stairs to my apartment. I bumped my nose on the door. It was locked. Malone had to remind me to secure the place when we left. He was laughing softly as he took the keys from my hand and unlocked the door.

"You still live close enough to the big city that you

should always lock up."

"Yes sir," I said, rubbing my nose. I walked several steps inside before I realized he wasn't behind me.

"Hey, Malone."

"Been a long day, Jamie."

I came back to the door. "And a lovely, relaxing one at that, but it's not that late. Come in."

He hesitated. "I don't want to rush things, Jamie."

I don't know if he could hear it, but my heart was thumping so loudly it could have stopped traffic on I-275. And that's three miles away. "C'mon, Malone. Stay for a while."

He hesitated again. My mind raced through all of the things I had done in the past to scare guys away. Being pushy or too easy was one of them. Attacking them in the hallway was probably another. But I really wanted him to stay. I couldn't tell if he'd made up his mind or not, so I jumped right in.

"Look, Malone. I'm not a kid. Neither are you. I'm not some cop-groupie. We're both adults. We've met half a dozen times or more. We've talked, gotten to know each other a little. We've just spent a lot of time together over the last two days. We've got a lot…"

Somewhere in the middle of this speech, he stepped into the room, pulled me close and kicked the door shut behind him. Then his fingers were caressing my face as he leaned in close for a kiss.

"Jamie," his voice was a soft, sexy whisper.

"…in common."

"Jamie," he repeated, gently kissing my mouth.

"Hmm."

His lips traveled down my neck. "Sometimes…"

"Hmm."

He was working his way back toward my ear. "You talk too much."

The first time on the sofa was wild. There no chance for foreplay. We both wanted it too much for that.

Clothes were flung so far I didn't find my red bra until two days later. It must have bounced off the wall and slid behind the planter. After the initial rush, Malone introduced me to the romantic aspects of each room in my apartment. At one point after a warm bath together, I was on my stomach in bed and he proceeded to drive me crazy by slowly making patterns down my spine with one solitary fingertip.

Each time after the first started out slow and tender. A kiss here, fingers stroking there. Malone was toying with me, bringing me to the edge of excitement now, his lips following his finger. My whole body felt alive, energized with the reactions to his touch. I groaned as he inched lower. His hands were on my hips now, his tongue flicking across my tailbone. With a magician's flick of the wrist, he rolled me onto my back. Before I realized what was happening, his face was sliding between my thighs. I had to clench my teeth to hold back the scream as his tongue worked its way inside me.

If I was tingling before, I was on fire now. The intensity of oral sex always surprises me.

My hands clutched his head. I realized my hips were thrusting, matching the rhythm of his tongue. His hands were grasping my buns so tightly I'd be able to fit into tighter jeans in the morning… if I survived the night.

I peaked. Delightful spasms wracked my body. I relaxed my grip on Malone's hair, expecting him to slowly rise from his position and scoop me into his arms.

But he didn't stop. He shifted, changing the angle of his lips and tongue, and kept going. His kisses were rapidly driving me crazy. Within seconds, I peaked again.

And again.

And, God help me, again.

Finally, when I was about to pass out from lack of oxygen, Malone withdrew. He kissed his way up my body, taking his time. A nuzzle here, another tantalizing kiss there. My skin was singing. My face was flushed, probably as red as my hair. At about the time I could actually feel my body starting to recover, he zeroed in on my breasts.

Now I can't say this is true for all women, I can only speak for me. Maybe it's because of the infrequency of romantic interludes. Or maybe it's my age. Or maybe the moon was rising.

My breasts are small. I hinted at that before. There are fourteen-year old girls out there with bigger breasts than mine. To clarify the situation, all my bras are padded and yes, the cup size is A. I don't know if that's good or bad, but it's what I've got and I'd never consider surgery to pump them up. All I know is that when Malone starting stroking and kissing my breasts, it's like there was a direct connection down below. I was immediately wet with anticipation yet again.

"What am I going to do with you," I whispered, my voice little more than a feathery gasp.

He paused in his efforts, raised his eyes until they met mine. "Whatever you would like to do. I'm open to suggestions."

"I'm the one who's open. Oh boy, am I open."

I pulled him up, coaxing him with arms and legs. Somehow I managed to confirm he was wearing a condom. Then our lips met as he slipped inside me again.

* * * *

I couldn't speak for Malone, but it was the most intense evening I had enjoyed in a very, long while. Okay, ever. I lost all track of time. All I knew was that it was pitch black outside and the rest of the apartment building had long ago gone quiet.

I was wrapped in his arms. He was on his back. My head was resting on his chest and I could hear the slow, steady beat of his heart. He sighed contentedly.

"Hey, Malone."

"Hey, Jamie."

"Aren't you glad I talked you into staying?"

"Mmm."

He twisted his wrist and peeked at his watch.

"Don't even think about it, Malone."

"Think about what?"

"About leaving. That would ruin a perfect date and it's no way to start a relationship."

I could feel his chest moving with a rhythmic laugh. "One date does not a relationship make."

I pressed closer against his chest. "Technically, it's been two dates, Saturday for the Italian dinner and Sunday for the magnificent brunch."

"Technically speaking, it could be one long date."

"Un nuh. You went home. Alone. Changed clothes. Came back several hours later. That just shows you recognized how special our date was. And you couldn't wait to come back to see me again."

I could hear the air moving through his lungs as he laughed.

"Guess you're right, Jamie. But just to get things straight, I wasn't thinking about leaving."

I burrowed closer. "Good answer, Malone. Do you have to work tomorrow?"

"You mean Monday tomorrow or Tuesday tomorrow? It's already one-thirty."

"Monday tomorrow."

"Afternoon shift starts at three."

I smothered a yawn into his chest. "Wake me around noon for breakfast."

CHAPTER SIX

I awoke to sunlight streaming in my face, feeling far from human. It was after noon. Malone was gone. Before I could feel sorry for myself, I heard him. Or more precisely, I smelled him. He was in the kitchen, cooking. I pulled on jeans and a Dolphins jersey and padded out to greet him. My legs felt like they weren't hooked on properly.

"Hi." My voice wouldn't work above a whisper.

"Hey, Jamie." He swept me up in his arms and covered my face with kisses. He was barefoot and bare-chested, wearing only the jeans from yesterday. Probably couldn't find the rest of his clothes.

"Whatcha making?"

"French toast with strawberries. Want some?"

"Uh nuh. I need coffee."

He guided me to a stool by the counter and fetched me a mug. One of my black leather boots was caught in the leaves of a huge Boston fern near the counter that divides the kitchen and living room. I had no idea where the mate had ended up, nor did I care. Noticing my red panties dangling from the bookcase caused me to blush for only a moment.

I was leery about eating Malone's cooking, until seeing

the food on his plate. Before Malone finished two bites, I moved my stool closer to his and let him feed me. No sense in dirtying two sets of dishes. I felt considerably better as breakfast settled in my system. Our antics last night had probably burned off ten thousand calories. At least, I hoped they had. I seldom eat meals as nourishing or bountiful as I had the last two days. It's more in my nature to be a nibbler.

"Any plans for today?" I asked. His bare skin was warm to the touch. I toyed with a nasty-looking scar on his biceps I hadn't noticed before. I must have been preoccupied.

"Nothing important. I'll go to the gym then get to the post by two-thirty. How about you?"

"I've got some revisions to do on a feature and there's always research." I leaned over and kissed a tiny bit of strawberry off his lip. As I moved, Malone's hands slid up my back, underneath the jersey. "Why, Sergeant Malone! You can't be serious."

"No ma'am. The mind is willing, but the flesh is…" he hesitated, searching for the right word, "tender."

I sighed in relief. "I couldn't agree with you more."

* * * *

That evening, I ran out to get some groceries. Malone promised to call me during the week and I wanted to be prepared to cook dinner if he was available. With his schedule, dinner might be eight or nine o'clock at night. I didn't want to stick around the apartment, or I'd be wondering why he didn't call. Malone didn't strike me as the type of guy who wouldn't call, though.

It was on the way home from the market that I noticed something. It took me five miles down the road and two James Taylor songs before I realized the importance of what I'd seen. I spun the Honda around and hurried back to the grocery store.

It was still there in the middle of the lot, an old red Mustang with splotches of gray down low on the fenders. Some of the splotches were small, like the size of a good snowball. Others were watermelon shaped. While I sat there, with the heater blasting, I watched a kid who looked barely old enough to be out after dark without his mother climb behind the wheel and roar out of the parking lot.

That disrupted my reverie and got me going. I zoomed back to the apartment and dumped the groceries on the counter. Pawing through my notes, I couldn't find the damn number. It's pathetic when you have to call information to get the number to the police. While trying to connect with him, I managed to get the perishables into the fridge.

I finally got him on the line. His voice was crisp and clear, all business. "Sergeant Malone."

"Hey, it's Jamie."

There was a lengthy pause. It was obvious he wasn't expecting me to call him at work. I jumped into the gap.

"Malone, it's about the shooting."

"Something wrong, Jamie?"

"Nobody's found the mystery truck, have they?"

"No, but these things take time."

"Do you remember what Smitty said, about the dog?" I asked.

"He said he was shot by a dog. Everyone figured it must have been the shock." Malone covered the mouthpiece of the phone for a moment. "He was in a lot of pain. Nobody expected him to make perfect sense."

"I think I know where the truck is."

* * * *

I'd persuaded Malone to pick me up after his shift. It was easier to show him than to explain it over the phone. He'd driven to the scene of the shooting, calmly listening to my theory. Now I wondered if he was just humoring me.

Still, he followed my directions to the junkyard. There was a full moon, but the clouds kept peeking around it, shrouding the night-light. We left the Cherokee and moved to the gate for a better look. Malone shined a big flashlight through the fence. Brutus trotted up to greet us, growling and slobbering all the way.

"What are you getting at, Jamie? You think this dog shot Kleinschmidt?" Malone started to rest his fingers through the fencing, then after a closer look at the dog's teeth, he tucked his hand safely in his pocket.

"No, but I think the truck is here. Or at least, it used to be here," I said.

"Not sure I understand what you're getting at." Malone's look told me I *was* right. He was humoring me.

"Let's come back in the morning. Just be patient until then."

"Whatever you say. Should I take you home now?"

Hooking my arms around his neck, I pulled him close. "Let's go to your place. My neighbors will get suspicious if I have a man around two nights in a row."

Malone smiled, those blue eyes sparkling. "You'll have to keep the primal screams down. One of my neighbors is in her seventies. When you get loud, you might just give her a heart attack."

"Or ideas."

His arms were around my waist. Bending down slightly, he moved in and let his lips find mine. With his arms supporting me, he dipped me backwards like a slow motion dance step. We kissed. Long and hot. Eventually he straightened and pulled me upright.

I could hardly catch my breath when we separated. "Better hurry up, Malone."

"It has been a very long day. As much as I would enjoy the pleasure of you in my bed, I'm bushed."

"You could have fooled me with that kiss. What do you have in mind, Sergeant?"

"A long, hot shower, followed by the two of us wrapped in a heavy down comforter. Then curled up in a very dark room where we can keep each other warm and comfy for at least six hours. From there, who knows?"

It was a very appealing image. "You expect me to believe that you won't try and take advantage of me in a situation like that?"

"I could just drop you at home."

I leaned up and gave his cheek a quick kiss. I could feel the stubble of his beard on my lips and realized I liked it. "I think I'll take my chances with the shower and the comforter."

We walked back to the Jeep. It was a good thing we'd been necking outside— it would have been impossible to drive with the windows fogged up. I hadn't made out in a car since high school, but the memory still brought a smile to my face. I could picture a little backseat passion with Malone without any problem.

His apartment was twenty minutes away. I noticed he kept trying to stifle a series of yawns. Once inside, I pushed him toward the shower. I hesitated for a moment, debating on the sanity of what I was doing. When I heard the water running, I peeled off my jeans and sweater and slid into his bed.

A moment of doubt raced across my mind. Behavior like this isn't my style. I've always been slow to take the initiative when it comes to sleepovers. Yet, here I was wearing nothing more than a silk camisole and panties, a splash of perfume and some earrings, in the bed of a man I hadn't known a month ago.

Before I could talk myself out of it, Malone stepped into the room. He pulled some shorts from a drawer and stepped into them. His hair was still damp when he climbed in beside me. He smelled of shampoo and toothpaste. Despite his claims of exhaustion, I could feel his body respond to the proximity of mine. Nature was obviously taking its own course. My body had been anticipating this since that kiss.

I moved with him, reveling in the feel of his warm skin against my fingers, my arms, my legs. The silk of the camisole felt like it was melting wherever it touched him. Suddenly I wanted to feel every inch of my bare skin against every inch of his. Oh, such blissful, heavenly contact.

"You remember what I said about sleep?" Malone began to cover me with kisses.

"Yes. No. This is crazy, Malone."

He pulled away, but not very far. "Want me to stop?"

I pulled him back. "What the hell."

The kisses continued. Somehow beneath the warmth of the comforter, his shorts and my panties disappeared. My camisole occasionally got bunched up above my breasts, but Malone seemed to be enjoying the wonderful softness of the fabric. I pushed him onto his back and slowly kissed my way down his body. Last night it had been his turn to take the lead. Tonight, it was mine.

* * * *

In the morning I curbed my physical cravings long enough to get dressed and drag Malone out of bed. I wanted to get back to the junkyard before it was busy. Malone didn't talk much on the way there. He wasn't sullen or angry, just tired. Exhaustion will do that to anyone. What I started last night took hours to finish. I'm not complaining, just bragging.

Joe Garibaldi greeted us at the gate as he was locking Brutus away. Only after Malone promised to keep his badge in his pocket did I introduce him.

"Malone's going to help me look for the kind of truck my uncle's got. He's more familiar with it than I am." I gave Garibaldi my best innocent maiden, damsel-in-distress look. Maybe I should bat my lashes more often. "Okay if we walk around, Joe?"

"Just watch your step. Brutus doesn't always crap in the same spots." Garibaldi laughed and went back into the office.

"What are we looking for, Jamie?" Malone asked as he checked the soles of his shoes. Garibaldi's warning had been a little late.

"A spotted pickup truck. C'mon, Malone."

"These were brand new sneakers," he mumbled.

"I'll buy you another pair. Quit stalling."

"Before or after you buy breakfast?"

"After." The offer of food had been the only incentive to successfully pry him out of bed.

We walked through the maze of dead automobiles, going slowly. Some of the stacks were leaning precariously to the side, tempting gravity. Malone steered me toward the middle of the path. Occasionally we heard the rustle of rats scurrying between the iron carcasses. How Garibaldi and his crew ever found anything amid this jumble was beyond me. There wasn't one simple row running between the cars. The paths twisted and swerved into little alleys, utilizing every available space on the lot. Despite having refrained from actually making contact with any of the wrecks, I had the uncontrollable urge to wipe my hands on the seat of my jeans.

Near the back of the property, I stopped in midstride. Malone had been studying the cars on the left and not paying attention to me. We collided and he almost knocked me into a fresh mound of dog shit.

"What's the matter?"

"Shot by a dog," I whispered. "There it is."

On top of a stack of three other pickups was the old Ford. The body was tan, not white, but it was spotted along both rear fenders and the tailgate with black primer.

"A Dalmatian," I whispered in awe.

"Son of a bitch," Malone muttered.

We walked around the stack as best we could, studying the pickup as it rested on the pile. There was no license plate on it, but I was positive this was the same truck. If I lived to be one hundred, I will never forget it. Malone took my hand and led me back to the office. Joe Garibaldi was watching a morning talk show, staring intently as the female guest discussed transsexual husbands raising children. He barely looked up when we stood before the counter.

"Use your phone for a minute, Joe?" Malone asked.

"Help yourself. Find something you can use?"

"Yeah, I think we did." Malone was strictly business. I was about to say something when he stopped me with a look. So, I played the role of dutiful woman and waited while he made his call. When he was done, he took my arm and led me outside.

"Nowalski is sending down a forensic team. One of the guys on day shift is going to get a warrant. Once we get inside the rig, we can check for evidence. "

"Then what happens?" I asked.

"Depends on what we find. Garibaldi can show us who brought that truck in, and when. That should give us another lead." Malone shook his head slowly. "You came through again, Jamie."

I didn't know if it was admiration or amazement in his eyes. Either one could work in my favor.

Three hours later we watched a wrecker tow the pickup truck out of the junkyard. The forensic team had done a preliminary search, looking for fingerprints and clues. Malone used the court order to impound the pickup for a more thorough search. Garibaldi released it without a word, a copy of the warrant clenched in his hand.

"Tell me about the truck, Joe," Malone said calmly.

"Normal routine, Sarge. I don't accept any vehicles without the title. Once a rig is scrapped, we note it on the paperwork, and keep it on file." Garibaldi tried to look calm, but his hands kept giving him away. They were trying to squeeze the letters off the warrant. If brute force could have done it, the page would have been blank.

Malone rested his elbows on the counter. "So how come you don't have a title for the truck?"

"Beats the hell out of me!" Garibaldi snapped.

Malone tried a different approach. Even though he was off duty, he was the officer in charge. No one else approached Garibaldi.

"How many guys work for you, Joe?"

"Ten all together. I got three full-time, the rest scattered through the week. Mostly kids." With an effort he put the warrant on the desk. The talk show was gone from the screen, replaced by the midday news. Joe switched the set off in disgust.

"What about at night, Joe?" I asked.

"We don't take any cars after hours. All the wrecker crews know that. If there's an accident, most vehicles go to the impound yard until the insurance guys get hold of them. We've never had a problem before."

"Couldn't somebody bring a truck in during the night?" Malone asked. He was watching me, instead of Joe.

"They'd never get past Brutus," Garibaldi insisted.

"What if they knew the dog?" I hinted.

"Like the kids who work for you?" Malone said.

"None of my guys will go near Brutus," Garibaldi said stubbornly. "The only one he listens to is me. That's why he stays in the cage during the day. We don't want him chewing on the help."

Malone stared at me and shrugged. I went outside and walked around. Adjacent to the junkyard was a cluster of trees on an undeveloped lot. A large wooden sign listed the dimensions and the number to call for anyone interested in purchasing or developing the land. A path was worn along the trees, leading back into denser foliage. I walked along it, hands jammed into the pockets of my leather jacket. Call me Ace Richmond, Private Eye, solver of crimes, finder of clues. Who needs a smoldering cigarette and a revolver jammed into a shoulder holster? Not me. I should have felt proud of myself for figuring out where the truck was, but it still might not lead us to who shot Kleinschmidt.

There were a number of empty beer cans and footprints in the dirt, as well as tire tracks. No bad guy was hiding in the shrubs, conveniently watching the action. This was probably the warm weather hangout for the guys from the factories lining the main road. Maybe I should stick to my regular line of work. I wandered back to Malone's Jeep and leaned against the rear bumper, staring at the pile of sulking iron wrecks. After a few minutes, Malone joined me.

"Do you believe him?" I asked as he slumped beside me.

"Yeah, I don't think he knows how the truck came into his yard. He's even willing to take a polygraph test." Malone stifled a yawn with the back of his hand.

"So how are you going to learn anything else from the truck?" I almost felt sorry for his lack of sleep. Almost.

"That's hard to say, Jamie. We'll run the vehicle identification number through the computers and find out who owns it. Then we wait to see if forensics turns up anything else." Malone bit back another yawn. "Look, I need to grab a nap before I report for my shift. Otherwise, I'll be a zombie tonight."

I slid off the bumper and stood before him. "I'm good at napping. Got all A's when I was in school."

He hugged me. "I'll bet you did. But..."

"What about my butt?" My arms went around his waist. I could feel the handle of his gun in the holster at the back of his jeans.

"I like your butt..." His right hand slid down and gently squeezed my bottom for emphasis.

"Good answer." I rewarded him with a kiss on the cheek.

"If you come with me, I'll never get any sleep."

"What about breakfast? You never did get your free meal."

Malone kissed the top of my head. "I'll take a rain check."

CHAPTER SEVEN

Since Bert knew I was working on the story, I thought I might be able to pump him for information. I offered to treat him to lunch. That was probably my first mistake of the day. He knew right away I wanted something. But Bert agreed to meet me at the Kabob House, the Mediterranean restaurant a few miles from the post.

Bert selected the best booth in the restaurant. He congratulated me on figuring out where the truck was. He was impeccably dressed as always when at work. Today he accented his navy blue suit with a bold tie, filled with bright colors and graphic designs. Bert ran his finger down the menu, making little check marks as he came to different dishes he had tried and liked. I let him order for both of us. Hummus, salads, grilled chicken with rosemary and garlic, coffee.

"You look good, Bert. New suit?"

"Nah, old suit, new tie. What's going on?"

"Can't a girl comment on your wardrobe? You always take such care in how you dress. A lot of men don't go to the trouble." I stirred my coffee and tried to keep a straight face.

Bert sat there with his hands folded until he had my full

attention. For a moment, I was thirteen again. "Jamie, I've worn suits to work since before I knew you. I buy maybe three a year. Geoffrey Beene. Blue, black and gray, sometimes a pinstripe. Shirts are always white, with a button down collar. If I want to add some flash, I pick out a Pangborn tie, like this one. We never bother with idle chitchat. So I repeat, what's going on?"

I started to respond with a typical wiseass answer. Then I stopped. Through all the years, Bert had always been there for me. After I moved out of the house, after college, even after Vera left him. He didn't even contest the divorce. And here I was, trying to manipulate him. I realized how low that made me.

"I'm sorry, Bert."

He flexed his hands open at the wrist, as if waving off my apology. "Don't apologize, Jamie Rae, just level with me."

Another memory from my teens raced through my head. "Guess I owe you another kiss, huh?"

Bert snorted that laugh of his. "I haven't heard that in years. How many are you up to now?"

I hesitated, looking up at the ceiling as though pretending to do the math. "Three thousand seven hundred and … eighty-four."

From the time he'd married Vera, Bert treated me like an adult. He was interested in everything I had done each day. We used to talk as we walked through the neighborhood during the evenings, catching up with each other. One night I apologized three times in a short span. That's when he pulled me up short and said, "Stop saying you're sorry and level with me. Each time you say you're sorry, you owe me a kiss." He'd tap his cheek and wait for a peck. I hadn't thought of it in a very long time.

"Over three thousand kisses from a beautiful young woman. Now that's something an old man could certainly look forward to."

A reprieve came in the form of the food. We ate the

appetizer without further conversation. Bert was patiently waiting for me to start. He looked like he could sit there through the entire meal without uttering another word and it would have no effect on him whatsoever. Men. So I used the time until the salads arrived to put my thoughts in order.

"This whole thing with Kleinschmidt is bothering me," I said at last.

Bert nodded slowly. "That's understandable, Jamie. Some officers go their entire career without ever pulling their gun. They never get involved in a shootout. Never end up in the hospital. Never shed blood."

"But it's not the shooting per se. It's his reaction. Why does he hate me?"

"Who said he hates you?"

The words were now coming out in a rush. "Bert, he won't even talk to me. I didn't hurt him. I didn't shoot him. I just happened to be there. I was only trying to help."

"So just because he won't talk to you, you figure he hates you. C'mon, Jamie, be reasonable."

"I thought I was."

Bert slid his salad bowl to the side. "Look, I can give you a dozen reasons why he doesn't want to talk to you and any one of them could be right. Or none of them. But it shouldn't matter. You can't always have it your way, Jamie. Life doesn't work like that."

"But Bert..."

The waiter appeared with the entrées. Neither of us spoke until he'd moved on. Bert's eyes locked onto mine. "Jamie, for as long as I've known you, it's always been full speed ahead. Whatever the prize is in front of you, that's what gets your attention and you won't take no for an answer."

"I'm not that stubborn..."

"Bull. If it weren't the Irish heritage, the red hair would be enough. It was cute when you were a kid, but you're not a kid anymore. You need to find a balance."

"What are you talking about?"

He took a moment to taste the chicken before answering. Nodding, he gestured with his fork for me to sample it. I knew he wouldn't answer until he was ready. The chicken was moist and tender. Better than I could ever hope to make.

"Life is a balancing act. It's all about finding the middle ground between the personal and professional sides of your life."

"Look who's talking," I snapped defensively. I wanted to reel the words back in the moment they were out of my mouth. Bert merely winked at me.

"See, there's that Irish temper. You don't like what you hear, you get defensive."

"C'mon, Bert, I'm not that bad."

He sliced another piece of chicken and popped it into his mouth. I had to wait while he savored it before hearing his response. "I didn't say it was bad, Jamie. Just that it's you. There is no middle ground with you. You do need to find that balance."

"But, Bert…"

"Think for a few minutes. Eat your lunch. Don't talk, just listen. You are a bright, beautiful young woman. You have talent. You've got a good heart and you care for people. Once you let them in. But you tend to bury yourself in your work. And before you compare us, there are a couple of things you probably don't know. Like the fact that I go to the gym about three times a week, partly to work out but also to socialize. I go to the theater about six times a year, with a very nice lady…"

My eyes widened but he cut me off before I could open my mouth.

"…this is not your concern. And there are a few other activities that I have, like a golf league in the summer, a billiards league in the winter. It gives me a sense of balance, between personal and professional interests."

"So you think I don't do enough for myself?"

"I think you try. But you get nervous."

Lunch was finished and we sipped coffee as the plates were cleared. Sometimes I forget how well Bert knows me. Maybe I try too hard when it comes to dating. If I can keep Malone interested, when do I tell Bert? And if I can't keep his interest, am I just proving Bert's point? .

When we were alone, Bert reached over and squeezed my hand. "Look, I think you're great. You have a lot to offer someone in a relationship. But Vera's track record probably scares the hell out of you. She's been through more marriages and relationships than a Hollywood actress. But that's her, Jamie. Not you."

"But what if it's hereditary?"

He snorted that laugh and shook his head. "Not a chance. You need to experience life, Jamie. Don't be afraid to let someone into your heart. It might just help you find some of the balance."

"But what if I fall in love with the wrong guy?"

"Jamie, we don't have any control over who we fall in love with. All we can do is let it happen and if we're very very lucky, they end up loving us back. That's just part of life."

* * * *

I didn't hear from Malone until Wednesday afternoon. There had been nothing in the papers or on the news about Smitty's case. Not knowing what was happening made me irritable. The least Malone could do was call. What an ingrate! Dammit, I'd found that truck! The last thing I wanted was to look anxious and start hanging around the station like a groupie. My stubborn streak prevailed. At last I got the call.

"Hey, Jamie."

His deep voice tickled my ear on the phone. "Hey, yourself. What's happening?"

"The truck you found was reported stolen over a year ago. The last owner died about the same time."

"Was he shot?" I asked.

Malone chuckled softly. "Heart attack. The guy was in his eighties. Nobody noticed when the truck disappeared from the old man's driveway. He was a loner, never had many visitors, or friends."

"What about forensics?"

"Nothing definite yet, except several strands of blonde hair. There's no telling exactly how old they might be."

My knowledge of forensic work is pretty limited. "Can you match the hair to the shooter?"

"It's possible. But first we need a suspect. A DNA comparison would have to be done. Right now, all we know is they were found in the truck. They could have been the old man's girlfriend or a kid he picked up hitchhiking."

"Not much of a lead," I said.

"Finding the truck was quite an accomplishment. You should be proud of it."

I shrugged away the compliment. "Catching the bad guy would make me proud. Finding the truck was a fluke."

"Better leave that to us, Jamie. I wouldn't want anything bad to happen to you."

I did a lousy impersonation of Scarlet O'Hara. "Why, Sergeant Malone, I didn't know you cared."

"Shucks, ma'am. T'weren't nuthin." He covered the mouthpiece and said something I couldn't hear. Then he was back. "Got to run, Jamie. I'll call you."

"Bye, cowboy." But he was already gone.

After I talked to Malone, I went to visit Kleinschmidt at the hospital. I didn't care if he wouldn't talk to me. At least he'd see me and I could see him. We nearly collided outside the door of the physical therapy room. I'd forgotten he'd been discharged last week and was surprised to see him, especially in jeans instead of a hospital johnny.

"Hey, Smitty. How's it going?"

"Hello, Jamie," he said woodenly. His right arm was still in a sling, and he shifted it around, trying to make it comfortable.

"Anything I can do for you? Buy you dinner? Any place you like," I offered.

"No thanks. Just leave me alone." He turned away and started down the hall.

"Did you know they found the truck?" I called after him.

He stopped and turned back to face me. "Yeah, Captain Nowalski called me Tuesday morning. But they haven't learned anything from it. I'd just like to forget it ever happened. Get on with the rest of my life."

His statement puzzled me. "How can you do that, Smitty? How can you forget being shot? About losing the use of your arm?"

He covered the gap between us faster than I would have thought possible for a guy his size. With his left hand he clutched my coat, and dragged me to the wall. Smitty jerked me up until we were face to face, my feet dangling in midair.

"Let it go, lady. I can't be a cop anymore. That's all I ever wanted to do. I don't care about anything else. They'll never find out who shot me. I just want to get better. I want to get on with my life." Smitty's face was only inches from mine. I could smell the anger seeping from his pores. I tried my best not to look scared.

"Put me down, Kleinschmidt," I pleaded. Where were all the nurses and orderlies when I needed them?

"Leave me alone. Forget about me." He shook me once against the wall, as easily as snapping a towel. My head thumped on the plaster and a thousand little stars began to dance before my eyes. He was starting to make me mad.

"Let me go, Smitty."

"What's going on down there?" A nurse the size of a battleship appeared at the end of the corridor and headed our way.

Kleinschmidt relaxed his grip enough for me to slide down the wall until my feet touched the floor. Then he pushed away from me with a scowl on his face.

"No more. Don't bother me no more."

He stormed away before I could regain my composure. The nurse hooked an arm around my waist and guided me to a chair. She brought an ice pack for my head. I had to wait until my vision was clear. Only after I recited the alphabet backwards did she agree I wasn't injured.

Stumbling out the door, I struggled to figure out what had just happened.

* * * *

Early Thursday afternoon, Malone invited me over for lunch. He cooked almost as well as he made love. Almost. He made broiled chicken, roasted potatoes, salads and lemon chiffon pie. I felt embarrassed at my own meager culinary talents. We didn't talk about anything relevant until after we were sprawled on his sofa. It wasn't as plush as the aunt, but it was still pretty cozy.

"I hear you visited Kleinschmidt," Malone said as he snuggled beside me.

"Good news travels fast."

Malone kissed my ears. "I understand it wasn't all good news."

"He's so damn angry. I was just trying to be his friend. Why did he have to be so rough?"

"He's a private guy. Kleinschmidt wants to be left alone with his troubles. He'll work them out, just him and his girlfriend."

"Maybe I could talk to her. She might tell me if there's anything I can do."

"I think you're trying to make something happen because you need it, not because of Kleinschmidt," Malone said.

"Now you're a psychologist on your days off?" I found

a finger stroking my cheek and turned to nibble it.

"Only on special occasions, like when the potential fringe benefits are right." His other hand had magically gotten under my sweater and was caressing my lower back.

"You think I wanted Smitty to get shot, so I'd have something spectacular to write about?"

Malone was trying to distract me with his attentions. He was doing a pretty good job of it too. "What happened is not your fault, Jamie. If you hadn't been with him, Smitty might be dead. Why don't you let it go?"

"I can't. I don't know why, but I just can't." His kisses were making conversation extremely difficult.

"You can play 'what if' until next Thursday and it's not going to change things."

"What do you mean?"

Malone pulled me closer, if that was possible. "What if Smitty wasn't on duty that night? What if a local cop had cruised through there first? What if he took a more direct route back to the freeway? Or what if there was some other traffic on the road?" He paused to kiss his way down my neck to my collarbone. "Get the idea?"

Talking was becoming impossible. Thinking was about to give way to pure animal reactions. My own body was rapidly responding to Malone's attentions. I shifted, pressing my hips against him and confirmed that his body was definitely aware of mine. "Uh huh."

"Put your mind to work on something else," Malone suggested as he nuzzled my neck. "I'm sure you can think of something."

Any further attempts at discussions faded rapidly. "What the hell."

CHAPTER EIGHT

The next day I went to the mall to pick up some supplies and look for a new pair of winter boots. I was rounding the corner by the sporting goods store when I saw Kleinschmidt. He hadn't seen me, but there was no mistaking his bulk and the sling on his arm. His good arm was draped over the shoulders of a blonde woman. She was probably his girlfriend.

Don't ask me why, but I spent the rest of the morning following them. They wandered through the stores buying clothes suitable for a camping trip, and a pair of hiking boots for her. My luck was running hot because they had parked two rows from my car. I followed them home. Smitty parked his Explorer in a carport, beside a motorcycle covered with a heavy tarp.

I remembered Smitty talking about going camping and hunting with his girlfriend and some of the trips they were planning. When they entered an apartment building, I ran up to check the mail slots. Two names were on the second floor apartment box, Kleinschmidt and Hatcher. Maybe they lived together, or maybe Smitty had a roommate. I walked back to my Honda, and was about to leave, when the blonde girl came back out. She wore jeans and a down jacket and a pair of bright red sneakers. She took the Explorer and drove away, so I followed her.

"Might as well see it through," I mumbled to my reflection in the rearview mirror. Talking to oneself is okay. Just ask any psychiatrist. Some will even tell you it's a sign of intelligence. Answering yourself, though, gets you a windowless room in the psychiatric ward with nice padded walls.

She cruised down the road, taking the corners fast and swung the Explorer into a saloon parking lot about three miles away. It was a place called Point, a favorite hangout of factory workers and bikers. She ducked into an employee entrance only a few feet from where she'd parked. I went through the front door and checked the place out.

There was a large wooden bar running at least forty feet, with vinyl stools neatly spaced along the counter. A quick examination of the room showed about thirty tables and a dozen booths. There was a riser at one wall with the setup for a band. Right now there were sixteen customers in the place. I realized the two waitresses and the bartender were only wearing bikinis and heels. Feeling about as comfortable as a preacher, I moved toward the vacant end of the bar.

The bartender had large breasts that defied gravity. Colorful tattoos decorated both arms. "What can I getcha?"

"White wine?"

She choked out a laugh and rested her palms on the counter between us. "Honey, this ain't the Whitney. We've got ten kinds of beer and hard liquor, but no white wine."

"Beer."

She sighed and raised her brows. "Want me to name them all?"

I shook my head and leaned forward. "What kind do you drink?"

"I like Sam Adams."

"Why don't you get one for each of us?"

"The boss won't let me drink on duty. But you can tip me the price of one."

"Done."

In a blink a cold bottle appeared before me. I placed a twenty on the counter and nodded at it. The cash disappeared in a flash.

"I'm Audrey. Who might you be?"

"Jamie. I'm looking for someone."

"Ain't we all, darlin'."

I smiled. "Not like that. There's a woman came in a few minutes ago. A blonde, she used the employee entrance. I think her last name might be Hatcher."

"What do you want with Melissa?" Suddenly Audrey was giving off vibes like a protective mother.

"I'd just like to talk to her about her friend Kleinschmidt."

She relaxed. "Damn shame about him. He's a nice guy. Came in all the time when he wasn't on duty. He met Melissa here. You're not a jilted lover, are you?"

"No, I'm just a friend. Can I see her?" I slid another ten onto the bar and watched it disappear.

"I'll send her out."

Two minutes later Melissa Hatcher came out from the kitchen area and took the bar stool beside me. She was about my height, maybe a little shorter. Her features were plain. I got the sense one of her eyes was slightly off center. She was wearing a bright blue bikini with a pair of golden slave sandals. Her legs were thick and muscular. I noticed several tattoos on her legs and hips. It was hard not stare at them. This was not the type of attire I expected for November.

"Can I help you?" she asked pleasantly.

"I'd like to talk to you about Herman Kleinschmidt."

Her eyes clouded as she looked me over. "Who are you?"

"Jamie Richmond. I was with Smitty when he got

shot."

At this comment her face paled. "So you're a cop?"

"No, I'm a writer. I was observing Kleinschmidt during his shift, gathering material for a magazine article and a book I'm working on. Guess I was in the wrong place at the wrong time. Can we talk for a minute?"

"What do you want from me?" She remained defensive, staring through me.

"I want to help. I feel sorry for Smitty..."

"He doesn't need your pity."

I nodded, raising my hands defensively. "Poor choice of words. Bad enough he gets shot and may lose the use of his arm permanently, but getting laid off at the same time really complicates things."

"So why do you care?" Melissa wasn't going to make this easy. She folded her arms over her ample breasts and glared at me.

"I don't know what else to say except I'm sorry it happened. I've tried talking to him about it, but he keeps pretending I don't exist." This was frustrating. "I just want to be his friend."

"Look, if that's what you really want then leave him alone. Smitty's the strong, silent type. He keeps things to himself. He doesn't want a lot of sympathy or attention."

I got to my feet. There was something unnerving about her. "He told me you two were planning a trip soon. Are you still going?"

"Yeah, we leave next Friday."

"You're sure there's nothing else I can do for him?"

"I'm sure. He'll work it out. He just needs time."

"If he changes his mind, or if you want to talk to me, I'm in the book."

"I'll remember that." Melissa's voice softened a little, but she still seemed uncomfortable talking to me. "Hey, Smitty will be okay. You just wait and see." Melissa saw Audrey signal her. "I've got to get ready for my shift. In an hour this place will be jumping with horny guys. And the more they drink, the better they tip."

I left the bar and walked back to my car. Deep down, I had a hard time believing her. Why would she lie to me? For that matter, why would anybody?

Okay, so maybe I'm just a little bit naïve.

* * * *

I fell asleep on, or more precisely, in, the fluffy sofa, watching an old Humphrey Bogart movie. As I drifted off, Bogey was arguing with two police detectives about his partner's untimely demise. My subconscious went for a cruise and drifted back to the night of the shooting. I was helpless to stop Smitty from being shot again, but this time I saw something I'd overlooked before. The arm holding the gun wasn't brown; it was a jacket sleeve. The glove on the hand was black. Something dangled off the sleeve of the jacket and it took me a moment to recognize it. Fringe. I'd had a suede jacket when I was in junior high, with strips of leather fringe along the sleeves and in rows across the back.

I woke up and struggled out of the clutches of the cushions. That style of jacket had been making a fashion comeback in the last year. A lot of people were wearing them now, and it wasn't going to help track down the guy who shot Smitty. Another fabulous clue brought to you courtesy of Ace Richmond, Private Eye.

Malone was working and hadn't called me. I felt sullen and disgusted with myself. Here was a guy I hardly knew, getting my emotions all mixed up, while visions of another guy haunted my sleep. If only Kleinschmidt wasn't trying so hard to tune me out. Maybe he was having problems adjusting to the injury and my appearances rekindled the trauma. Maybe it irked him that I had been there to help. Could Kleinschmidt be such a Neanderthal that he was embarrassed about being saved by a woman? Could his frail ego have been crushed when he was shot in front of me? What if I hadn't been there and nobody came looking for him? I grabbed the phone and called the station.

"State Police, Trooper Rand."

"Is Sergeant Malone in?"

"Yes, ma'am, hold please."

I tried to be patient, but it seemed like two hours passed before there was a click on the line.

"This is Malone."

"It's Jamie."

"Hey, Jay, what's up?"

"Just wondering how you're doing. What time does your shift end?" I realized how desperate that sounded after it popped out of my mouth.

"Couple of hours. You okay?" His soft tones warmed me. I'd never known anyone who could have that effect on me.

"Yeah, kind of lonely." Where the hell did that come from?

"I could stop by," he said.

"No, I don't want to bother you, Malone."

"No bother at all. I was going to call you in the morning anyway." Chills of anticipation tickled my spine.

"I'll leave the door unlocked."

"Great. Listen, I have to go. Someone just brought in a kid driving a stolen car."

"I'll be here, Malone."

"Bye, Jamie." There was click and he was gone.

I couldn't believe what I'd told him. And I never had the chance to ask the question I'd called about. I trudged into the bathroom and took a good, hard look at myself in the mirror. My eyes were bloodshot and puffy, my shoulder length red hair was sticking up every which way, and what looked like a zit was forming on my chin. Swell. I was wearing sweat pants and an old Tigers shirt. Bring on the glamour photographers. One look and Malone would go running for the hills. Forget the fact that we'd been pawing each other like a couple of hormone-crazed teenagers for the last couple days.

A long, hot soak in a bubble bath would help. But first, I decided to shave my legs. I took my time, careful not to nick those troublesome spots around the ankles. I can get by with shaving once a week, but I had noticed Malone's reaction to freshly shaved legs before and the way he likes to kiss them. Once the shaving was done, I filled the tub and slid beneath the bubbles. I scrubbed my chin until the pimple was gone, washed my hair, and put some drops in my eyes. A little perfume behind the knees and ears made me feel more feminine. A little more on the neck was helpful too. And, yes, a quick spray before I pulled on some black silk panties that were trimmed with lace.

I put fresh sheets on the bed then turned the lights down low. In the bottom of a drawer filled with slightly torn stockings, I found a lacy black negligee my mother had given me last Christmas. I'd never had an occasion to wear it. From the kitchen I got the Dutch oven and filled it with ice. There was most of a bottle of Beringer white wine in the fridge, so I jammed that deep among the cubes. I took two wine glasses out of the cupboard and saw a bright red smudge of lipstick still on one.

By the time I washed the rim and carted the wine and glasses back into the bedroom, Malone was due. The down quilt warmed me as I slid beneath the covers to wait. I was hoping he wouldn't be forced into working overtime.

The bedroom door creaked open and he stepped inside. He moved so quietly that I hadn't heard him come into the apartment. Malone's smile was wide and his eyes were dancing as he sprawled on the bed beside me and gave me a smooch.

"Hey, Jamie."

"Hey, Malone. Want some wine?" I jerked a thumb at my makeshift ice bucket.

"Maybe later," he said as he kissed my eyelids. "How was work?" I gasped.

"Fine." His lips were slowly covering my face. His skin

was soft and smooth. He must have shaved when he changed clothes. Malone was on to something. There really is something incredibly sexy about freshly shaved skin.

"Anything exciting?" I whispered.

"No."

"You sure?" It was suddenly very warm under the quilt.

"Jamie?" He was still kissing me.

"Yeah?"

"Hush."

"`kay."

After the first time, we curled together, sharing one glass of wine. And here I'd gone to the trouble of washing both glasses. Malone took one melting ice cube and rolled it down my face, cooling the skin. He held it against the hollow in my throat, and let the water drip its way onto my chest. A trickle slid between my breasts as he began to slide it along my body.

"Where did you learn how to do that?" I moaned.

"St. Valentine's Church."

"Yeah, right."

He stopped moving. "I'm serious. A woman I used to date worked at the church. She taught me the ice cube trick. Cools the skin but gets the spirit hot."

"You're terrible."

He moved the ice again. "Why?"

"Talking about another woman when you're in bed with me." I pretended to be angry with him, but Malone wasn't fooled.

"You sounded upset when you called," he said, deftly changing the subject.

"The deal with Smitty still bothers me. I even had a dream about the shooting. Now I'm starting to wonder if I'm imagining things." I burrowed close and felt his arms encircle me. Nice. I didn't even wonder where the ice cube ended up.

"What kind of things?"

"I think the driver of the truck was wearing a leather jacket, one with fringe on the sleeves."

"Fringe?"

"Yeah, strips of leather. It's decorative."

He gave my ass a playful slap. "I know what fringe is."

"It doesn't mean anything. There must be a million jackets like that in the city. And I'm not even sure my subconscious didn't make it up."

"Hmm." Malone smothered a yawn.

"You shouldn't be tired, unless you're getting old," I teased. "What time did you start work? Three, maybe four in the afternoon?"

"I had to be in court at nine this morning. Then the captain had a staff meeting at one o'clock, and my shift started at three." He paused and kissed me. "It has been a very, long, day." I was rewarded with a kiss between each word.

"I'm surprised you had any energy left for me."

He flashed his low wattage, killer smile. "It's amazing how the proper motivations can recharge my batteries."

"Are you working tomorrow?" I already knew the answer. I was just trying to keep the conversation going. I wanted him to stay.

"All weekend. I have to be on duty at three. Guess I should be headed home." He made a half-hearted attempt at getting out of bed.

"Stay. We need to talk."

"I'm beat, Jamie. Can it wait 'til morning? "

"Sure." I dragged him back down beside me. "But I still want you to stay."

"I could never refuse the wants of a lady."

I batted my lashes at him. "And if the lady wants more?"

Malone rolled onto his back, pulling me on top of him. The rat must have been feigning tired, because he was certainly ready. "Then the lady gets more," he whispered as he slid inside me.

His lips on mine silenced any further conversation.

* * * *

It was after ten when we went out for breakfast. My cupboards were barren. I promised Malone I'd go grocery shopping today. Over waffles and bacon he caught me staring at him. I was having grapefruit and coffee. I was willing to control one appetite while the other was being satiated.

"What's on your mind, Jamie?"

"I don't know where to start."

"Make believe it's a book. Try the beginning."

I laughed. "I never start at the beginning. I usually work from the middle, then write the ending and work backwards."

"Okay, start in the middle." I noticed the twinkle had returned to his eyes when he smiled.

"Let's start with you. Do you realize, it's been two weeks since we've been seeing each other, and I know more about my dry cleaner than I do about you?" I swiped a piece of bacon from his plate, hoping he wouldn't notice.

"What do you want to know?" He motioned the waitress over to refill our coffees.

"Everything, Malone, I don't even know your first name."

"What's in a name?" His eyes were turning me on, making it difficult to sit still. "Does it really matter?"

"I guess not."

He chuckled. "How about if I give you a profile? I'm forty-two, divorced, no kids, like skiing, sailing, baseball and football. I've been a state trooper for seventeen years and never wanted to be anything else. I like classical music but not opera, jazz but not reggae. Don't even mention rap. I prefer to sleep in the raw. I drink coffee black, without any fruity flavors in it. Good enough?"

Some profile. My character sketches are more detailed

than that. "For now. But you still didn't tell me your name."

"I only use Malone. Your turn."

"For what?"

"Your profile. Pretend it's for a famous magazine ad." He held his coffee cup in both hands as he sipped, letting the steam rise before his eyes.

"Okay. I'm thirty-one, never been married, seven kids by seven different men, I like opera and reggae and some rap. I like almost all sports. I have a degree in journalism. All I've ever wanted to do is be a writer. I don't even know where my diploma is. I'm a packrat, but when the seasons change, I make it a point to throw stuff out, like old boyfriends, and get organized."

The look on his face was a cross between disgust and humor. "Rap music?"

"Some of it's good."

"How'd you get the scar on your stomach?"

"Appendix burst when I was a kid." I got serious after the waitress cleared away our dishes. "Tell me more about work. How long have you been on afternoons?"

"Three years. I like it. We can request any shift every three months, depending on seniority. I prefer the afternoon slot. It gives me the mornings and early afternoons free. Sometimes we work seven or eight days straight. But every third weekend, I get four days off in a row." Malone settled back against the chair and watched me.

"What about court appearances?"

He shrugged. "We go whenever the judge requests us. There is overtime pay for anything not part of your regular shift."

"What was the big meeting about yesterday with Nowalski?" It felt funny referring to Bert by his last name. As far as I knew, Malone was still unaware of my relationship with his boss. For now, I wanted to keep it that way.

Malone's eyes narrowed slightly. "You don't miss much, do you sister?"

"Not if I want to do my job well. Can you talk about it?"

He relaxed and shrugged again. "Don't see why not. Governor Aikens sent out the new plan for the posts yesterday. In the past, each location has been open around the clock. If you were involved in an accident during the day and stopped in at three in the morning, you could get a copy of an accident report. Now, he's closing some posts down."

"Closing them completely?" I was surprised.

Malone sipped his coffee before answering. "The governor's plan is to close the outskirt locations during the evening. They will be open during the day, from 8:00 A.M. to 5:00 P.M. Beyond those times, they will be closed."

"Are you saying there won't be any cops in those areas after the posts close?" This sounded crazy to me.

"Relax, Jamie. Patrol cars will continue to make their rounds. Communication will be handled by radio with several main base locations. Our base will control all contact with seven different posts. Each one will be on a different radio frequency."

This sounded expensive to me. "So how does this help the budget? And what happens when the system breaks down?"

"When a post was open all night, there were five troopers on duty inside. Now, those five will be freed from the paperwork duty and sent back on the road, where they can do the most good."

"Which is why some guys with low seniority, like Smitty, will get laid off?"

"Right. Troopers with more years in were relocated to different posts." Malone signaled for the check. "This sort of thing happens all the time in other businesses. Law enforcement's no different."

"What about you? Will you be transferred?"

"It's doubtful. I've been here so long I'm part of the building. Occasionally I'll drive a patrol car, splitting station duties with two other sergeants. The governor doesn't want to disrupt everything; he's just trying to make us more cost efficient."

He sounded calm about the whole program. Perhaps nothing rattled Malone. "I guess it makes sense. But what about people you arrest during the evenings? If there's no one at the station to watch them, what do you do with them?"

"Good question. There's always a city or township police department nearby. If we have a prisoner, like a drunk driver, they will be transported to the facility where the arrest was made."

"So the cars are still on the streets, making the rounds, but the stations are all locked up."

"Basically, that's it. It eliminates the need for five men to be holding down the fort. Communications is still done by radio and the dispatchers have a computer system that can locate a residential address and give the trooper directions if needed. It's as fast as it ever was."

"Who will be manning the communications?"

"Right now we have troopers doing it, because they are more familiar with the system and the calls. Eventually, they plan to train civilians to handle it. That will help put more troopers back on the road too."

"Or lay more off," I said sullenly.

"It's possible. Look, Kleinschmidt may be recalled if he regains the use of his arm and can pass the physical exam. But he's still drawing full pay while he recuperates. Until the state has a balanced budget and can afford to pay more troopers, we have to make do with what we've got." Malone finished his coffee and got out of his chair.

"I know, but I still don't like it."

He flashed me that gentle smile.

"Neither do I."

CHAPTER NINE

We were driving back to my place after brunch when I remembered why I'd called him last night.

"When Smitty got shot, what would have happened if I hadn't been there to call it in?" I asked.

"There isn't much traffic on that stretch of road, especially at night. If nobody came along, it could have been an hour before the communications officer would have noticed anything wrong."

"An hour! That's crazy, Malone."

"Look, Smitty was still conscious. He could have used his portable radio to call the post. There's a repeater in the car, on the same frequency as the regular radio. He could have called in if you didn't."

"Don't you check on your guys more frequently?" I was stunned by such a lackadaisical approach.

"No need. During the course of a shift, they normally call in about every ten or fifteen minutes with requests anyway. If it's a slow night, the dispatcher can make contact every half hour. It all depends on what's going on." Malone stopped at a light and turned to face me. "Why the sudden concern?"

I lowered my eyes. "Guess I worry about you."

He grinned and leaned over to kiss me. It was one of those slow, languid, lingering kisses I liked so much. Behind us a horn sounded as the light turned green. "It's been a long time since anybody worried about me."

"Don't mention it." I faced forward, blushing, as the car behind us honked again.

I knew Malone was right. There were systems in place to keep the troopers safe, protocols and people. All well trained and thoroughly tested. So why was I worried? Was I getting in over my head with Malone? Or was there something else?

"Why so serious, Jamie? You look like you're trying to find the answer to double digit inflation."

I smiled softly. "Just working on a part of the book. I get ideas at the strangest times."

Now it was his turn to smile. "I'll bet you do."

* * * *

Saturday night was made for frumping. I kept my promise to Malone and went grocery shopping, restocking the cupboards and the fridge with all kinds of goodies. Chocolate chip cookies, macaroni and cheese, tomato basil soup and olives were my gourmet dinner. Before he went to work, Malone made a derogatory comment about my pedicure, which still showed chips of polish from my vacation six weeks ago. I wedged cotton balls between my toes and waited for the neon pink polish to dry. The phone rang as I settled in my rocking chair.

"Hey, Jamie."

"Hey, Malone. I decided I'm going to find out what your first name is. If I guess, will you tell me?"

I could picture his smile coming across the line. "Sure."

"Busy night?" I lounged back in the chair, draping my legs across the arm of the aunt. It would have been impossible to paint my nails on the sofa, no matter how comfortable it might be.

"Actually it's kind of quiet. I wanted to tell you about the truck."

"Kleinschmidt's truck?" He had my attention.

"I remembered what you said, about the fringe on the jacket. So I pulled the lab report and went back over it again." Malone was calm, as if he were describing the weather. I wanted to smack him.

"What did they find?"

"Lots of smudges on the wheel, mirrors, door handles and gear shift, but nothing we could match to any records in the computers."

"Go on," I said anxiously.

He ignored my prodding and kept talking in a bored monotone. "Anyway, among the items found in the truck were two narrow strips of leather. One was only an inch long, the other closer to three inches. They were snagged on a spring that poked through the seat cushion."

"That's it?" What a letdown.

"Yeah, that's it. No way to tell if those belonged to the driver or not. But if the jacket he was wearing did have fringe on it and the strands caught on the spring match, we could use that as evidence."

I bent over my toes and blew on them to speed up the drying process. "Whoop-de-doo. You still don't have anything of consequence, Malone."

"Maybe not, Jamie, but if we get a lot of little details, they may add up to enough someday. I just thought you'd want to know. What are you doing?"

"Sitting here stark naked with the stereo on. I'm in the mood for some reggae music. I couldn't find any opera that I liked. "

His voice went softer on the line. "Mind if I stop by after work?"

"I'd mind if you didn't."

"See you around midnight," Malone said.

Since I'd opted for neon pink polish, it only seemed appropriate to continue with that color scheme. Once my toenails were dry, I painted my fingernails as well. Every now and then, when I feel the need to splurge, I go to a salon for a real manicure. Since I spend a lot of time on the keyboard my nails take a fair amount of abuse. It just isn't practical to have them very long. But I like to paint them occasionally.

One night, last week, Malone had let slip that he had a soft spot for pink. I'd been waiting for an opportunity to see just how much of a softy he was. So in addition to my nails, I dug out some appropriate sleepwear. I don't have a huge supply of slinky negligees. With the colder weather, I usually wear flannel pajamas. Not exactly the wardrobe of choice to spark romantic interest. But I knew there was an item that would fit the bill tonight.

In the bottom of the drawer was just what I was looking for. Probably the most money I've ever spent on myself for something I'd only dreamed of wearing before. Actually, I've worn it twice, but never when I was expecting a visitor. It's pure silk, in a very soft shade of pink, with thin spaghetti straps at the shoulders. It hugs my meager curves very nicely and stops about mid-thigh. It dips very low in the back, so if I'm feeling extremely naughty, I can always wear it backwards. The gown comes with a matching wrap, the same shade of pink with a little black trim along the collar and the cuffs. The wrap drapes to my ankles.

I wanted to get Malone's attention from the moment he walked in the door. With that in mind, I searched the closet for a particular pair of shoes. They were black, with very high heels and open toes. I slipped them on and posed before the mirror. I sure hoped Malone had been taking his vitamins.

He was due any time now. I wanted no doubt in his mind what this evening had in store. The stereo was ready with a variety of discs, some soft sultry ballads by Diana Krall, James Taylor and light jazz instrumentals. There were candles lit, both in the living room and the bedroom.

I touched up my makeup, just lipstick and a little bit of blush. A quick spray of perfume and I was ready.

I was heading for the windows to see if I could spot his car, when the door opened. Malone stood there for a moment, not moving. I couldn't see his eyes clearly. He was in that shadowy area, just inside the door and all the candles were behind me. My heart did a little stutter. Was I coming on too strong?

"Hey, Jamie." His voice was a hoarse whisper.

"Hey, Malone." I wanted to pose for him in some seductive way, but I was frozen in place, halfway between my bedroom and the aunt.

He just stood there, staring at me. His head moved slowly. I could feel his eyes tracing their way down my body. A chill ran up my spine, but I still couldn't move. Then I heard a clicking noise and realized he had managed to close and lock the door behind him. At last he moved.

"You are an incredibly beautiful woman."

I blushed and lowered my eyes. "It's just the gown."

"Don't do that." His voice had taken on a thick, husky quality.

"Do what?"

"Downplay the compliment." Malone reached out his right hand and took my left. Then he turned me and we started dancing slowly, moving in perfect sync to the music. I think it was Krall singing "The Way You Look Tonight". "Just smile sweetly, say, 'thank you' and accept the fact that I believe you are an incredibly beautiful woman."

I was having trouble finding my voice. "Thank you, kind sir."

He twirled me around the apartment. It amazed me how well we moved together. With the heels, I was almost eye level with Malone. His right hand was now inside the wrap, resting lightly on my bare back just above the edge of the gown. "Do you have any idea how incredibly sexy this is? To come in that door and find you like this?"

"Do you have any idea how sexy you make me feel, Malone?"

He stopped moving at that moment and dipped me, just as the song ended. "I've never had that effect on any woman before. At least, not to my knowledge."

"Malone."

"Yes, Jay?"

"Are you going to kiss me?"

That killer smile crossed his face. "I thought you'd never ask."

* * * *

Sunday morning, Malone took me to the target range. I had never fired a gun before and was curious. Besides, it was a good excuse to be with him. I watched him practice with his service piece then asked to try it. He attached a fresh target to the line and sent it out into the range. Then he gave me a lesson.

"This is a 9 mm, semi-automatic Sig Sauer. It's made in West Germany, and it has a sixteen round clip. Add one more in the chamber and you're good for seventeen shots."

Malone eased a fresh clip into the handle of the gun and knocked it home. With a fluid motion he pumped a bullet into the chamber, which he referred to as "racking the slide". Then he stood behind me with his arms extended and let me hold the gun. His hands gently locked onto my wrists and he steadied my aim.

"Don't jerk the trigger. Try to squeeze it slowly, take up the slack a little at a time," he suggested. His breath was warm on my ear.

I did as instructed and jumped when the gun went off. I missed the target by a mile. He'd made it look so easy when he was doing the shooting.

"Hold the gun a little tighter. It won't bounce so much when you fire. Take it slow and easy."

This time I braced my feet and rested my weight against Malone. When I was ready, I tugged the trigger and sent two shots toward the target. Both hit the paper, but missed the outline of the body.

"Not bad," Malone said, letting his hands fall to his side. "Try it on your own."

By the time I fired off the whole clip, my shoulders and arms were tingling. The 9 mm packed quite a kick. I had hit the target nine times, actually striking the figure with four. Gingerly, I handed it back to Malone. He replaced my target then sent his out beyond where mine had been. Smiling, he reloaded the clip and stepped back up to the firing line. Using just his right hand, he leveled the gun and shot it, steadily spacing out the shots until the clip emptied. Then he pressed the button for the target to return. I was stunned by his accuracy. Four holes in the heart, four in the forehead, two where the nose should have been. Three shots in each shoulder and one in the groin.

"Show off," I muttered.

"You just have to practice."

"How much practice did it take for you to get so good?" I asked as we drove home.

"A lot. I learned how to shoot when I was a kid and it carried over with the job. I practice about twice a month. I can do the same thing with a rifle."

Now that he mentioned it, I remember the small medals on the pocket of his uniform.

We got back to my place and Malone dropped onto The Aunt. He hooked my wrist with his fingers and pulled me down with him.

"Hey, Jay."

"Hey, Malone, how about Mortimer?" I'd been guessing names since his arrival last night. So far I had tried Johann, Albert, Wolfgang, Ferdinand, Marcellus and Siegfried. It had to be something unusual if he didn't use it.

"Nope. How come you never married?"

Embarrassed, I turned my face away. "I almost did."

"What happened?"

"The bachelor party. His buddies invited his ex-girlfriend to surprise him. They locked them in a hotel room, without any clothes on and didn't come back for them until the next day. By that time, they had fallen in love all over again."

"I'm sorry." Malone sounded earnest.

"Don't be. If he were that easily taken away, the marriage wouldn't have worked. Chances are, the first time he ran into somebody from his past, he'd be long gone. I'm better off without him. What about you, Malone?"

"I got married early. Fresh out of high school, I signed up for a three-year hitch in the army. Thought I'd see some of the world and get the money for college. Did my three years, came home and started school. We met in a calculus class in September. By Christmas break, we thought we knew it all. We got married over the holidays by a justice of the peace." Malone turned slightly on the aunt, and drew me into the circle of his arms. "Marilyn figured she'd convince me to go into business, instead of police work. When I joined the academy, she got cranky. When I graduated and was stationed over here, she refused to move. Marilyn didn't want to leave Kalamazoo and I had to go wherever they assigned me. We didn't make it to our three-year anniversary before we were divorced."

"Sorry it didn't work out." That was the longest, most personal speech he had given since I'd met him.

"Ancient history and it's probably for the best. Not everyone understands a cop's position. On any given night, you might be involved in a situation where you end up dead because of drunk drivers, drug runners, family disputes, car accidents, assaults. Anything can happen." He kissed the top of my head and ran his fingers lightly down my spine.

"Like Smitty?"

"Yeah, just like Smitty."

We were quiet for a while, just lying there together. I tried to block everything from my mind and focus on being with him. The silence slowly unnerved me. There were so many things about him I wanted to know, but I wanted him to volunteer the information instead of questioning him like an interview. Or how he might interrogate someone. Was I beginning to think like a cop? Maybe it wasn't such a bad thing.

"Where are we headed, Malone?" My fingers toyed with the buttons on his shirt. I couldn't look at his face for fear of his answer.

"Where do you want to go?" His arms were around me, his hands lightly stroking my back.

"Forward. But I don't want to go alone."

"Nobody does. It seems like we've been slowly moving along this path, enjoying the sights and each other's company. Are you in a hurry, Jamie?" His deep voice was throaty and gentle. When he spoke softly like this, I found it incredibly sexy. I realized he often used this voice on the phone. Now hearing it in person, with him holding me close, was rapidly turning me on.

"No. I guess we could just keep taking it slow and easy." I was trying to find the nerve to ask the next question.

"Just nice and slow, one day at a time."

"Have you been seeing anyone else?" Here's the part where I usually learn the bad news. Like, let's just be friends, no need to ruin a perfectly good relationship.

"I haven't dated anyone seriously in months." His hands continued to work their magic on my spine. "You?"

"I had a hot and heavy relationship with a carpenter in April. I interviewed him for a couple of articles. He was a runner up in archery for the Olympics and liked to do restoration work on old homes. It might have gone on longer except for one thing."

"What's that?" His cheek was resting on the top of my head. I could smell his cologne. It was gentle, not overpowering like some guys prefer.

"His wife. She was my roommate in college. They separated just before we started dating. Then they got back together. Guess you could say I drove him to her."

"Ouch."

I wanted to get back to lighter subject matter. Too much serious talk makes me nervous.

"How about Myron?"

"Not even close."

What could have been one of the last pretty days of fall was just beyond my window. The remaining leaves were dropping off the trees, inevitably finding their way to lawns freshly raked only moments ago. A soft breeze was blowing. The sun and a few clouds were playing a game of tag. The sun was winning.

We snuggled for a while, enjoying the contact. The Jewish Aunt was certainly weaving her magic spell. A pair of mourning doves (or maybe they were love birds) perched on the limb beside my balcony. Bombs could have dropped in the hallway and neither one of us would have budged from the couch. My phone rang twice and I made no attempt to get it. That's why I have an answering machine.

For a big guy jammed against the back of a fluffy sofa, Malone showed amazing dexterity in the art of clothing removal. He didn't fumble with the snap on my jeans or the clasp on my bra. They just seemed to vaporize at his touch. I ended up on top, completely undressed, breathless. The ridiculous vision of my mother overseeing this scene and nodding her approval dashed through my mind.

Malone worked two fingers under my chin, raising my face so I'd look at him. "You really worry about me?"

"Sure. You're a nice guy, Malone, even if you don't have a first name. I've just never dated a cop before."

"And I've never dated a reporter before, or a writer. I keep fighting the urge to search the room for a hidden recorder."

"Relax. I don't use one. I've got a pornographic memory." I slithered up and started nibbling his ear.

"You mean photographic."

"You do your thing, I'll do mine."

CHAPTER TEN

Malone went to work Sunday afternoon. I was scheduled to be in New York on Tuesday to meet with my agent and the publisher's editors. Monday, I ran around town doing errands and trying to keep my mind off cops. Every time I let my guard down, Malone's image would slide behind my eyes and I'd get all fuzzy. While trying to concentrate on something else, I kept stumbling over Kleinschmidt. I couldn't shake the feeling I was overlooking something, so I went back to my place and did what I do to take my mind off things—write.

Every detail I could remember concerning that Friday night went into the computer. From the way Kleinschmidt first reacted, up to the time Malone dropped me off at the post. I used my notes to prod me along whenever I slowed down, but one glance was all it took to bring the evening sharply back into focus.

I wrote about Smitty's mannerisms. The methods he used to check license plates on cars we were following to verify they weren't stolen. The way he approached a car he stopped; always in profile, keeping the majority of his body out of the driver's sight. The leniency he employed when dealing with a driver whose muffler was dragging the ground. The way Smitty listened to a kid's story and let him off with a warning instead of giving him a ticket for driving with a suspended license. Smitty even gave him a ride home. When I got to the part after dinner, prior to the shooting, I stopped to gather my thoughts. Something kept nagging me. I reread my notes, and then scrolled through the text on the computer. Acid exploded in my stomach when I read the line, "He always approached the car in profile, keeping the majority of his body out of the driver's sight."

When he'd stopped the pickup truck, Smitty had marched right toward the door. It was as if he wasn't afraid of the driver. Instead of moving slowly along the fender and keeping out of harm's way, he went right at him.

My mind would be on Kleinschmidt for the rest of the night.

* * * *

I was taking an evening flight into New York to discuss my book, rather than risk morning travel and be late for my meeting. I had plenty of time to get to the airport. As I was getting a Diet Coke out of the fridge, I saw a foil-wrapped chunk of steak leftover from last night's dinner. It would go bad before I came home Thursday and I was about to throw it out when inspiration struck. I took my suitcase and my shoulder bag out to the car, tossing the steak on the passenger seat. It was after seven when I got to the junkyard. Brutus was trotting around inside the fence, growling and snarling as my lights picked him out among the rusting remains. Who needs a more expensive security system to guard a bunch of wrecked cars?

"Hey, baby. Want a snack?" I left the motor running and approached the gate. The dog growled louder and pressed his snout against the chain link fence. I opened the foil wrapper on the steak and the growling stopped. He ran an obscenely long pink tongue around his teeth and began to pant excitedly.

"Attaboy, Brutus." I threw the meat over the fence and watched him chase after it. He caught it before it hit the ground and savagely ripped the foil away. With Brutus occupied, I got a chance to study the gate closely. The thick chain wrapped around the posts of the fence was new and shiny, but the padlock was old and weathered. Satisfied, I returned to the Honda and drove to the airport. Look out world, Ace Richmond, Private Eye was back on the case.

My flight to New York was uneventful. Other than two Marines who shared the seats beside me, no one tried to hit on me. Could everyone else tell I was no longer interested in strange men, or was I losing my appeal to them? I didn't ask. The Marines soon became busy with a magnetic chess game, working on moves I'd never heard of. I napped.

At the hotel, I received a very pleasant surprise. My agent, Shannon Ripley, had left several messages about meetings. I read them as the bellhop carried my bags to the suite. I know it's expensive, but my accountant tells me I can write it off my taxes. I hope he's right. There was a basket of fruit big enough to support a family of six for several days, and a vase jammed with fresh flowers. It was a beautiful bouquet with a single white rose in the center.

"Enjoy your stay, ma'am." He handed me my room key as I forked over a tip. I was tempted to stiff him. Maybe he was from the south, where proper manners required that you address a female as ma'am. But I was still young enough to be called miss. "Anything you need, Ms. Richmond?"

"A bottle of white wine would be nice, a Riesling or a Piesporter."

He nodded quickly. "Be right up."

I checked the card on the fruit basket. My publisher had supplied breakfast for the week. The flowers made me curious. A thick ivory envelope held the note, just four simple words, that quickly took my breath away. "I miss you. Malone." This guy sure knew how to pull my heartstrings. If I wasn't careful, I would end up writing romance novels.

Shannon Ripley came by for breakfast Tuesday morning. She'd taken the liberty of ordering a pot of coffee and a plate of chocolate croissants from room service. After dozens of telephone conference calls and three personal meetings, Shannon knows me pretty well. She gave me a friendly hug when I'd opened the door then followed me into the bedroom while I finished dressing. The waiter left the cart in the sitting room and almost killed himself trying to get one last look at Shannon. She has that effect on men.

"Such absolutely gorgeous flowers." Shannon bent over to sniff them, but she didn't fool me. I'd already tucked the card in my purse. "Secret admirer?" Shannon didn't pull any punches, which is one of the many reasons why I like her.

I waited until her reflection showed in the mirror. "New lover."

"I hope he's better than the carpenter. Really, Jamie, your taste in men often astounds me."

"It can't be jealousy, Shannon. I'm sure you get plenty of variety with all of your lovers."

"Variety can be extremely rewarding, you know, part of the spice of life. Especially if you can choose wisely." She sat on the wing chair beside the vanity and crossed her long legs.

Shannon's been my agent for two years. She knows everything about everyone in the New York publishing business and has never failed to get a client a respectable contract. In her early forties, she looks like she's thirty and dresses like she's nineteen. And she's got the figure to carry it off. With her chestnut colored hair dancing across her shoulders and soft brown eyes that look like coffee with a healthy shot of cream, she can stop traffic on the busiest street just by strolling along the sidewalk. She's also an inch taller than I am, but she wears a size two dress. When she's feeling flirtatious, she breaks out the spike heels and the short skirts.

"Don't talk to me about variety, Shannon. Last time I was in town you couldn't remember your escort's name." I put the final touch on my eye lashes.

"Shall we discuss business over coffee?"

We moved into the sitting room and shared our breakfast.

"What's Myerson want on the new book?" I asked.

"He'll probably want half a dozen concessions and a week of work on revisions. He'll cry you a river about the state of the economy and the declining market for mysteries. And since they have committed to your second book, he'll expect you to jump at whatever he says." Shannon sipped her coffee daintily and nibbled at a corner of her first croissant. I had already polished off two.

"Got a plan?"

She gave me the smile used by the wolf in *Little Red Riding Hood*. "Cite the real information on the market for mysteries along with the advance order from the three big retail outlets. Add that to the number of sales pending online and the fact that we've already obtained a bid for the paperback rights."

"So I'll end up with…"

"I'm thinking three days' worth of revisions and a better contract on your next deal. You are still pursuing the idea of a patrolman's duties?"

"Yes, I've been doing some research."

"I hope it's in depth."

I choked on my coffee.

"You could say that."

* * * *

Thursday evening, I returned to an unexpected heat

wave. My apartment was stuffy and quiet. I was reminded of a spinster aunt who spent her life cooped inside her little flat, afraid to venture out into the world. I threw open the windows and switched off the furnace. I'd taken nothing but business suits with me and was dying to get comfortable in a pair of jeans. I dumped the contents of my suitcase on the floor of the closet and was shucking my heavy wool outfit when the phone rang.

"Hey, Jamie. How was the trip?" Malone's deep voice cooed in my ear.

"It was good, Norton." I had decided to give him a different name each day I saw him or talked to him. Sooner or later, I'd hit the right one.

"Wrong again. How about dinner?"

"I thought you were working."

"I am. Cops have a right to eat too, you know."

I realized I was standing in front of the mirror, wearing nothing but stockings and high heels. I wondered if Malone would like the outfit. Maybe I should ask.

"So do you want to meet me or not?"

"Yes, Norton. Where?"

"O'Leary's in ten minutes?"

"I'm naked. Give me twenty," I said. If I told him what I was really wearing, he might break out laughing, or faint dead away.

"Forget O'Leary's. I'll be right there," he teased.

"Twenty minutes." I kicked off the heels and squirmed out of the stockings. I opted for a pair of very lacy panties with a matching black bra, and rummaged in the closet for a corduroy skirt and a cotton blouse. I called this my flirt skirt. It was knee length but had functional snaps that ran down the front of it. Depending on how flirtatious I was feeling determined how many snaps were left undone. I grabbed my bag and hurried off to meet him.

O'Leary's wasn't crowded when I arrived. Malone was in uniform, sitting at a booth near the back of the restaurant. He was talking with Sean O'Leary, the octogenarian owner. Sean gave my hand a gentle squeeze then toddled off to schmooze with his other patrons. Malone greeted me with a tender hug and a chaste kiss on the lips then pulled me in beside him on the bench.

"Saving it up for later?" I asked.

"Bank on it. How was the trip?"

"Okay. Shannon wants me to do a hundred pages of rewrites for the book and my publisher wants a synopsis for a series of mysteries we've been kicking around. If I can sell them on the series, I'll get an advance. We also talked about a promotional tour for next spring."

"Is that a big deal?" Malone asked.

"It could be, depending on the reviews. There may be twenty cities in the Midwest, with talk shows and autograph sessions. If they are footing the bill, it can help increase sales. I'll know more after the first of the year."

Malone opened his menu and scanned the page quickly. A waitress approached, wearing a green leotard and skirt with a black apron. He glanced at me and raised his eyebrows. "Want me to order for you?"

"Sure, I'm starving."

Malone turned to the girl. "We'll have the roast lamb stew, tossed salads with raspberry vinaigrette, and coffee." He looked at me and I nodded.

"You eat here often?" I asked as she wiggled away. I'd swear she put a little extra swing in her hips for Malone's benefit. I didn't know whether to be angry or jealous. Idly, I undid a couple more snaps on the skirt. It fell open to mid-thigh.

"Couple times a week. Sean's a decent guy. The food's good and the prices are reasonable. A lot of the guys stop in. The service is pretty good too." He winked at me. It was obvious he'd noticed the extra wiggle.

"You're a good guy, Norton."

He leaned over to kiss me. His left hand landed softly on my knee. I watched the expression hit his eyes as he realized this was a smooth bare leg he was feeling. Malone gently slid his hand a little higher. A shiver of excitement ran through me. It took several moments for me to withdraw from that kiss.

"Want to skip dinner?" I asked. I was glad this part of the restaurant was dark, since I was blushing beet red.

"I think we're going to need that nourishment for later." Malone reluctantly removed his hand from my leg.

After dinner he walked me out to the parking lot. He stopped beside my car and leaned against the door.

"Did I tell you how much I missed you, Norton?" I put my arms around his neck. His hands went to my waist.

"Nope."

"Would it be improper for a girl to kiss a cop while he's on duty?"

Malone's eyes went to his left wrist. "I've got two minutes before I check in."

He tipped his head down to meet my lips and kissed me warmly. If anyone was watching, I didn't see them. I didn't care. His left hand remained on my hip. The right had somehow drifted between my legs and undid two more snaps. The skirt was only fastened to the top of my hips now. A shudder ran through my whole body as his fingertips stroked me through the lace panties.

"Welcome home, Jamie." Gently he pulled away and straightened up.

"Thanks for the flowers. They were beautiful." I had given the bouquet to Shannon to brighten her office. The white rose, I'd brought home.

"My pleasure. Glad to have you back."

"How glad are you, Norton?"

"See you later?" he asked.

"Oh yeah. It may take me a while to be able to drive. And I seem to be having this problem with my door. It just won't stay locked at night." I pushed his hands away and stepped back before I attacked him in the parking lot.

"I'll have to see what I can do to remedy that. And Jamie…don't change your clothes."

* * * *

Things must have been quiet at the post, because Malone's shift ended at eleven and he was at my apartment by twenty after. I'd returned home and did a bunch of little things like going through the mail, paying my bills and cleaning the kitchen, trying to keep my mind off him. It wasn't helping.

He came into the room silently. I had a mug of tea and a fashion magazine on the counter before me. There was one lamp on low by the aunt. The rest of the room was in shadows. I didn't say a word. The look on his face said it all. There was something mischievous about his eyes I hadn't seen before. An old expression jumped to mind, something about the devil dancing in one's eyes. Malone crossed the room without a sound. I started to say something and he silenced me with a kiss, long, hot and deep.

He lifted me from the stool. I expected him to carry me to the bed, or maybe the aunt, but that wasn't in his plans. Malone placed me on the counter. Still kissing me, his hands went to the snaps on my skirt. Roughly he yanked the last two panels apart. I gasped in surprise as his fingers shredded the lace panties. Malone dropped to his knees, burying his face between my legs. I had to bite my lip to keep from screaming as I peaked. He must have been anticipating my reaction. Suddenly Malone rose in front of me. There was a thump as something solid hit the floor and then he took me, right there on the counter.

I dug my nails into his back and wrapped my legs around him. We had been spontaneous and intense before, but this time was putting me over the edge, fast.

* * * *

It was early Friday afternoon when Malone left me to

117

go to work. Teasingly, I asked if he was going to the gym for a workout. He chuckled, gave me a quick kiss then went to the post. I could personally attest to a cardiovascular workout earlier. We had collapsed around four and slept curled together under several heavy quilts until nine. Malone made coffee and helped me clean up the mess from our escapades. One, or both, of us had shattered my favorite tea mug. We had tipped over one of the plants. Pillows and cushions from the sofa were scattered about the living room. The remnants of my lace panties dangled from the rocker. I blushed when Malone found them, but stared in disbelief when he rolled them into a ball and tucked them in the pocket of his jeans.

It felt strange to think about the way we'd behaved. Suddenly I wondered if he hadn't been in uniform last night if we would have climbed into my car and had sex right there in the parking lot. Something told me it was entirely possible. Pushing passionate thoughts of Malone out of my head, I grabbed the phone and called Joe Garibaldi.

"Hey, Red, you still looking for a pickup truck?" he joked.

"Not really. But I did have a question for you. Have you ever had anyone break in or any vandalism at the yard?"

Garibaldi didn't hesitate. "Sure, we get a few problems every now and then, but nothing serious. Mostly it's kids trying to scavenge a few parts for some hot rod. The valuable rigs we keep near the back, until we dismantle them."

"Anything recently, like within the last month or so?"

"Well, we did have trouble one night," Garibaldi muttered.

"What happened, Joe?"

"Not much really. There's a security guard who works at the plastic plant across the road. He always stops down after his lunch, to give Brutus a treat. Guy's a retiree, doesn't have any family of his own. He only works to have something to do. Otherwise he'd go stir crazy. Me, I'd retire, work's the last thing I'm gonna do."

"Go on." I tried not to sound too anxious.

"Anyway, Barney, that's the security guard, he brought Brutus something to eat, like he always does. Only Brutus wasn't around. He called and called, but the dog wouldn't come. Barney thought maybe Brutus had trapped a squirrel back in the yard, so he left his food and went back to work. When Barney drove home that morning, Brutus was standing by the gate, like always."

"That's it?" I asked.

"Except the chain. Somebody snipped off my gate chain with a pair of cutters. They might have gone inside, only to be scared off by the dog."

"Was the gate open?"

"Nah, it was closed, just like always. Otherwise, old Brutus would have been off and running, looking for a little strange, if you know what I mean."

Memories of that obscene pink tongue flashed before my eyes. "I get the idea. Thanks, Joe."

"This about that old pickup the cops hauled out of here?" Garibaldi's voice took on a conspiratorial tone.

"Maybe. If I ever figure it out, Joe, I'll let you know."

CHAPTER ELEVEN

After five steady hours of concentrating on rewrites for my persnickety editors, I needed a break. Malone had fed me breakfast in bed, but that had been eons ago. All I'd had since then was a mug of Earl Grey tea. I left the apartment in search of something substantial and nutritious.

There's a little bakery down the block from my place, where they take huge chocolate chip cookies out of the oven and surround them with a heaping scoop of French vanilla ice cream. Then add gobs of hot fudge and more chocolate chips. So sinful. They even let you sit in the back, away from the store window, and devour it. I hadn't indulged in one in months.

I washed it all down with a cup of coffee and waited for my system to explode from the sugar shock. Surrounded by the aromas of bread baking and cinnamon rolls, I probably gained five pounds by osmosis. I wondered how long I could continue to eat like this before my figure went to hell. I'm not scrawny like a fashion model, but I am slender. I like the shape I'm in. And apparently, so does Malone. One of these days, I'll get back to my yoga classes.

After the feast I went for a long walk, bundled inside my down coat. Yesterday's heat wave had been Mother Nature's cruel trick. Today was typical November weather, cold and blustery with a snappy wind. Even in the frigid air, it felt good to stretch my legs and let my mind wander. I walked about two miles, circling back toward my apartment. As I approached my building, two people came out of the entrance and trotted over to the parking lot. I froze.

One of those two was Herman Kleinschmidt. Even if I hadn't been close enough to see his face, there was no mistaking his bulk. The right sleeve of his jacket flapped loosely at his side. His arm was still in the sling. The other person was nondescript, smaller than Smitty, wearing a nylon parka with a hood.

Don't ask me why I didn't hurry after them instead of stepping back behind an oak tree. Maybe it was something about the way they moved, or the way Smitty kept looking back over his shoulder. Either way, it made me uncomfortable. I waited until I saw them drive away together before I went inside.

My apartment building isn't fancy. It's part of a complex where six rental units make up each three-story structure. I've got the east side of the top floor, with a nice view of the park. I'm the only person who works at home. Chances were nil that Smitty was visiting one of my neighbors.

I'd been gone over an hour. Since I hadn't taken my car, I hadn't taken my keys, which meant I hadn't locked my door either. My heart was thumping erratically as I reached for the doorknob. The door swung open at my touch and I remained in the hall, afraid to go inside. Where the hell was Ace Richmond, Private Eye when I needed her?

When no one jumped out from behind the towering pile of magazines in the corner, I took a cautious step inside. Everything looked the same as when I left. The handmade quilt from my cousin Linda remained draped sloppily off the bentwood rocker. Someone could have been hiding inside the Jewish Aunt, but it would take them ten minutes to struggle free of the cushions. Okay, so I'm not Holly Homemaker.

I went down the hall to my bedroom. The blankets and sheets were in the same twisted clump I'd left them in after attacking Malone's naked body over the dirty breakfast dishes. My clothes from the New York trip still protruded from the closet door.

"Anybody here?" I whispered foolishly. I don't know what I would have done if someone had answered.

That left the bath and the spare bedroom. It's not really a bedroom, since there's no bed in there. I use it as my office. A desk, two file cabinets, a bookcase and some plants make up the majority of the furnishings. My computer dominates the room, with cables running everywhere. Printer, monitor and keyboard are perched precariously on various parts of the desk.

If I hadn't already been nervous, I certainly was now. My computer was on. Not just the hard drive or the monitor, but the entire system, even the printer. I never leave the system on. Call it being economical or superstitious or environmentally concerned, I don't care. I never leave the system on, because I never know how long I'll be gone. And I hadn't been using the printer. There's an independent switch for it, used only when needed.

"You bastard!" I slammed my hand on the desk. Too late now, I ran to the front door and latched the bolt. Then I grabbed the phone and started to call Malone. I got through six numbers before hesitation settled in. Nothing was moved. Nothing was stolen. What exactly did I expect Malone to do? Swoop over to protect me?

I went back to the computer and began checking the data. Every file I could remember was still there. I'd been working on the revisions earlier and all of my changes were intact. Nothing had been disturbed. What could he have been doing? I keyed in the directory and scrolled through a list of all my files. At first I didn't notice anything wrong.

I sat back and closed my eyes, concentrating. Like most writers, I use code names for the files in my computer. Since there's no master list that will reveal to anyone what each file actually contains, the only way to discover the contents to any particular file is to call it up on the screen. For the project I was considering about the state trooper, I had named the file Licorice. There's no connection between that and the story, it's just what popped into my head. Beside the file name is the size of the file in bytes, and the last dated entry. My system automatically creates a backup whenever a file is changed, sort of a fail-safe system. I hadn't been in the Licorice file recently. My first and only entry had been on Monday, before my trip to New York City.

But the directory showed activity today. The main file showed a slightly different number than the backup file. I swallowed hard and punched in Licorice.

Four pages of notes lit up the screen. There was my own unique style of speed typing for rough drafts. No care with regards to spelling or punctuation, just rambled lines of words with an occasional break for a new paragraph or thought. My notes ended in the middle of the fourth page. There was a gap of five or six lines then this message appeared.

LEAVE IT ALONE BITCH! IT'S NOT WORTH DYING OVER.

* * * *

Malone's tapping at the door roused me from the couch. He looked surprised when I opened the locks and let him in.

"When did you become security conscious?" he asked as he hugged me.

"Since about seven-thirty." I felt so much better with him here.

Malone held me at arm's length. The concerned look on his face made me feel even safer. What better protection could a girl have than her very own police sergeant?

"What's going on, Jay?"

"I'll show you. It's easier."

Malone looked over my shoulder as I keyed in the file name. I jumped to the end of the fourth page and leaned back so he could read it.

"What's this mean?"

"I didn't type it. Kleinschmidt did." He was no longer Smitty, the friendly trooper. He'd invaded my home. He'd played with my computer. I felt violated. I described to Malone about seeing him and someone else leave my building as I returned from my walk, and how I'd searched the place when I got inside. Malone turned off the computer and led me back out to the living room. We sat and let the Jewish Aunt push us together.

"Why would Kleinschmidt break into your apartment?" Malone asked.

"I don't know, Oscar. Maybe we should go ask him."

He gave me a brief smile, very low voltage. "He'd probably deny coming here. It would be your word against his."

"What about fingerprints?"

He shrugged. "Chances are, if he did leave any, you probably obliterated them when you went through the place."

I felt like a schmuck. "I should have thought of that."

"Forget it. Kleinschmidt would have worn gloves anyway."

"Why is he so upset about my story? I haven't even written anything yet, just a bunch of notes from the night we were on patrol." I snuggled closer to Malone, feeling his warmth through his sweater. "It's all in rough form, just observations. There's nothing worth getting angry about."

"Maybe you should forget it, Jay. It could have been Kleinschmidt's idea of a joke."

"Not funny, Oscar," I said into his chest.

"I didn't say it was."

Malone probably didn't enjoy Friday night very much. All I did was cling to him. I wasn't interested in sex, movies or anything else. I just wanted to hold him and have him hold me. Even when we woke up in the morning, I was still hanging onto him.

"Morning, Oscar."

"Not even in the right part of the alphabet. How you doing?" He was slowly sliding his fingers through my hair, letting my locks pass gradually between them.

"Better. Sorry I was such a sissy last night."

"Forget it. We can't behave like wild animals every night we're together. It was a nice change just to cuddle."

I peeked to see if he was serious. He was. "How did you ever get away from all the women in this town with an attitude like that?"

"Usually I have to beat them off with my nightstick," he said with a grin.

"Sounds too kinky for me. I thought cops were supposed to be macho men, able to leap tall buildings in a single bound?"

"Only when we're in uniform. We must follow the union's behavior rules. Cuddling is a violation of the by-laws."

"What's up today?"

"The usual grind. Work at three. My schedule's fairly open until then. Got any ideas how I should occupy my time?" He rolled onto his back, pulling me on top of him.

I pushed him away and slid out of bed. "Yeah. Let's go visit Kleinschmidt."

Cold rain was falling heavily, accompanied by gusting winds. The roads were slick and nasty. Already the forecast was calling for ice and mixtures of snow for the evening. I didn't envy Malone or the guys on his shift who would be out on the streets.

There was no answer at the apartment when we rang the bell. None of the neighbors were home either. Malone thumbed the button for the apartment manager and finally got a response. We went inside. The manager's rooms were on the first floor, at the back of the building. A scrawny man in baggy work pants and a worn sweatshirt poked his head out into the hallway as we came through the security door.

"No vacancies! The waiting list's been full three months now." His voice was high pitched and nasal, as if he'd been cheated out of puberty. I wondered when the last time he'd stepped out of that apartment and engaged in a real conversation. Probably back when Roosevelt was in office. Teddy Roosevelt.

Malone dug out his badge and introduced himself. The manager's demeanor changed slightly.

"Whatcha want?"

"I'm looking for one of my guys, Herman Kleinschmidt, from apartment 502. Seen him around lately?"

"Nah, I don't bothers people and they don't bothers me. But I did see his girl, early yesterday."

Malone looked at me.

"Melissa Hatcher?" I offered.

"Yeah, that's her. She said they was gonna be gone for a week or so, going off camping. Seems kinda late in the year for that, if you asks me," the manager said, wiping his nose on his sleeve. A class act.

Malone stepped a little closer to him. "When was this?"

The manager pulled back and used the door as a shield, impeding Malone's progress. "'Bout three. Said they was leaving right away. That's all I know."

Malone nodded and stepped back. "Thanks." The door swung shut before he could say anything else. We both heard the bolt slide into place on the other side.

"Now what?" Malone asked.

"C'mon, Oscar. I'll spring for lunch."

He slid an arm around my waist and hugged me. "There's nothing quite as refreshing as a liberated woman."

My taste buds were screaming for bagels and lox, or hot pastrami with crunchy dill pickles, so I took Malone to my favorite delicatessen. He eyed me suspiciously when we parked the car, but I refused to let him drive somewhere else.

"I've seen trucks bigger than this place," Malone grumbled.

"No derogatory remarks until you've tasted the food. By keeping the exterior grungy, it keeps the prices down."

"Great. You save money. I get food poisoning from Gertie's discount house of botulism."

I elbowed his ribs and marched inside. A heavyset woman with sparse white hair was behind the counter, beefy hands deftly wrapping a sandwich in thick waxed paper.

"Jamie! How come you stay away so long?"

"Hey, Toots. Meet Malone."

She stepped out and gave me a fierce hug and pumped Malone's hand vigorously. "Always glad to see friends of Jamie's. I hope you're hungry."

"Starved." I noticed Malone massaging his hand, trying to restore the circulation. "What's fresh?"

"Everything!"

I caught Malone's eye. "Do you trust me?"

"Mostly." There was a hint of uncertainty in his voice. The rat was using my own expression against me.

"Be that way."

He shrugged and moved down the counter to one of the high backed wooden stools. Toots wiped her hands on a fresh towel and beamed at me expectantly.

"Pastramis on rye with Swiss cheese and hot mustard, a

couple of old dills and two Cokes."

Toots shook her head. "The pastrami's gone. No more until Monday."

My mind whirled as my stomach groaned in disappointment. "Onion bagels with cream cheese and lox, capers and tomatoes on the side, coffee, black."

Another shake of the thin white hair. "No lox."

"You said everything was fresh!"

Toots grinned, revealing her mail order dentures. "Fresh out of lox, fresh out of pastrami, fresh out of ham."

I puffed a breath in desperation. "What do you have?"

"Lean corned beef on onion rolls with Munster. Roast beef with horseradish sauce on French. Smoked turkey with Monterey Jack and Bermuda onions on pumpernickel. Potato salad and new dills." Toots spread her enormous hands and shrugged in a form of apology. "It's been quite a week, and a very busy Friday. Who can predict these things?"

I sighed. "Roast beef, twice with Cokes."

Toots smothered me briefly in another hug and disappeared beyond the counter. I wandered down to join Malone. He was giving the place a critical inspection. There are no tables at Toot's, only twelve wooden stools beside the old Formica counter. Another counter runs along the window facing the street, but there's no room for chairs or any more stools. During the week it's not uncommon to see executives in designer suits standing beside deliverymen at the window while they scarf down Toot's fare. She decides what goes on each sandwich. Substitutions are forbidden. If you don't like turning over the controls to your meals, eat somewhere else.

"Where did you find this place?" Malone asked.

"I took a blood oath never to reveal the source."

He was about to comment when Toots emerged from the kitchen and laid two heavy platters before us. I can barely hold half of one of her sandwiches in both hands, so I knew Malone would not go hungry. He offered Toots a thin smile and she scooted away to take care of someone else.

"What is this?" Malone tentatively prodded his sandwich with a finger.

"It's food. Shut up and eat."

He was trying hard not to laugh as he lifted a corner and took a big bite. That was all the encouragement he needed. Between mouthfuls of succulent rare roast beef, we discussed the timely departure of Herman Kleinschmidt.

Just like his landlord said, the idea of camping at this time of year seemed ridiculous to me too. It was cold and damp no matter where you went in the state. Deer-hunting season started in less than a week, though. This was not a fact I knew, but one Malone explained to me. Thousands of people, not just cops, wait all year to take their vacations during hunting season.

"People actually live in tents when they do this?" I asked. The idea didn't appeal to me at all. Being frostbitten and wrapped in layers of nylon or canvas did nothing for my creature comforts. I prefer cotton and satin, flannel jammies and warm cozy beds.

"Some do," Malone said. "Most people use campers or stay in cabins. It depends on how rugged you are, and how rugged you want to be."

"How about you, Oscar? No desire to go traipsing through the woods, trying to kill innocent creatures?"

"No, but you've got the wrong idea about hunters. It's an opportunity to test their skills with their weapons, but they're also doing a service. The deer population keeps growing and there's never enough food for them to survive the winter months. By thinning the herd, it gives the others a better chance at survival."

"Sounds like you're justifying slaughter," I teased.

"It's more humane than letting them all run free and starving to death." Malone leaned back and folded his arms across his chest. "Besides, I like venison."

I polished off the last of the potato salad and tried changing the subject. "I always wondered why people would name their daughters Bambi, after the cartoon character. Bambi was a male deer, the young prince."

He relaxed. "Next time I meet a Bambi, I'll ask her. I would be willing to look around. For comparative purposes, I could do a survey. You could consider it research."

"Forget it. Research is my department. Ever go hunting?"

"A few times. But I never had any luck. Guess I'm too much of a city kid. How about you, Jamie? Any cravings to get away from the city and experience rural life?"

I smiled. "Only if we got a cabin with a big stone fireplace. That's one thing I wish my apartment had. I love to snuggle in front of the fire and watch the flames."

"Sure that's all you want to do by the fireplace?" Malone asked quietly.

"That depends on who I'm with."

CHAPTER TWELVE

By Thursday, I had nearly forgotten about Kleinschmidt's visit to my apartment and I was up to my eyebrows in work. Malone hadn't been around since Monday night, but he was coming up on four days off. I was trying to complete as much work as possible before he finished his shift tonight. He'd promised a romantic weekend I wouldn't soon forget, but the rat wouldn't tell me anything about it. I despise men who can keep a secret.

Late in the afternoon, I finished the revisions and called Shannon Ripley in New York. She suggested I email her my efforts so she could review them before sending them on to the publisher's office.

"How's the research coming on the new book?" Shannon asked.

"Good. I've been trying to work on that between shifts on the keyboard."

"How about the new lover?" I could hear a throaty exhale as she spoke. "Is he still curling your toes?"

"Are you smoking again?"

"Don't try to change the subject, Jamie."

"I'm concerned about your health." I could feel the warmth of embarrassment on my face.

"Fine," Shannon said. "I only smoke cigarettes at two times during the week. One of them is Thursday afternoons when I go over accounts with a glass of wine."

"And the other?"

A soft chuckle of laughter flowed over the telephone line. "You're a writer, Jamie. Use your imagination."

Now my face was as red as my hair. "I think that's more information than I needed to know."

"So what about your new guy?"

"Let's just say I haven't scared him off yet."

"Jamie, there may still be hope for you."

We talked for a few more minutes about the book and the revisions. Shannon commented on what a difference technology made, where I could send days' worth of writing to her office instantaneously. I remembered the first story I wrote for a high school newspaper on an old Royal typewriter. I can't image trying to write a novel that way. The revisions alone would be enough to discourage me. It helps you appreciate the dedication of writers from centuries ago.

Since last week, I'd made a conscious effort to keep the apartment locked. Even if I just went downstairs to check my mail, I began securing the door. Malone didn't say anything about my sudden precautions, but I think he approved. Earlier today I went to the locksmith and had copies made of the apartment keys. After making certain they worked, these went on a brass ring with leather tag adorning it. I wrapped them in a little box for Malone. Then I ran out to the liquor store for a couple bottles of wine. It started to snow as I was on my way home, the street glistening with little white sparkles. The phone was ringing as I came into the apartment. Malone.

"Hey, Jamie."

"How are you, Grover?"

Malone chuckled, warm and soft in my ear. "Where do you get these names?"

"I bought a baby book."

The chuckle died quickly.

"A what?"

"A baby book, with possible names in it. You know, like Grover means from the grove."

"Why did you need a book like that?" There was an obvious tension to his voice I'd never heard before.

"You asked where I was getting the names from. I scan the book and check off ones that might apply to you." Suddenly it dawned on me what he must have been thinking. "You jerk; you thought I meant *having* a baby." I couldn't help laughing.

"Yeah, guess I did," Malone said. I could almost hear the relief in his voice.

"Where would you get an idea like that, Grover? You know we've always practiced safe sex. Plus, I'm on the pill. And we haven't been intimate that long."

"Never mind. I don't like making a fool of myself. I just wanted to let you know I'd be late. I'm covering the first hour of midnight's shift for Sergeant Mankowski. His wife's in the hospital."

"Anything serious?"

"Appendix. She's in surgery now. The doctors keep reassuring Mankowski that it's a routine procedure. I'm betting he's still pretty anxious. He figures she'll be done in a couple of hours or so. Greenwald is coming in to pick up the rest of the shift. Mankowski wanted to come in when she's in recovery, but Captain Nowalski wouldn't hear of it."

That sounded just like Bert. Gruff on the exterior, but a big plush teddy bear on the inside. "I hope everything goes okay for the Mankowskis."

"Nowadays, an appendectomy is pretty standard. Probably even more so since you had yours done. Hey, maybe you and Carole can compare scars."

"You are a strange man, Malone."

"See you around one."

"I'll be here, Grover."

"Right. And Jay…"

"Yeah?"

"Keep the door locked."

"Bye, Grover."

I piled the pillows on the floor by the bay window and watched the snowfall. Something about the way snow shines as it falls pleases and depresses me at the same time. Fresh snow always seems so clean and fragile, as if it's giving the city a gentle bath. Here's a chance to hide all the filth and debris we leave behind, buried under a lily-white blanket. For some reason, tonight I felt like getting pleasantly buzzed. I warmed some apple cider in the microwave and added a healthy shot of Southern Comfort. Sitting like a sultan on the pillows, sipping my potent brew, I watched the snow. The heat from the booze warmed me and my thoughts turned to Malone.

I'm my own worst enemy when it comes to men. I meet a guy and my weird sense of humor tends to scare him off. Or it's my career. Or it's my body. I have always been slender and I don't have fabulous curves. I've got a small chest, narrow waist, small hips. There is nothing about my physique that would set the world on fire. Romance is something that happens to other people. I write about it only if I can work it into a story. But Malone…

Geez, what a difference he was. He seemed to like my body just fine. And he had me so wrapped up, I couldn't think straight. The other day I was doodling while on the phone with Shannon. When I hung up I almost screamed. I'd written "Mrs. Jamie Malone" half a dozen times in a notebook and circled it with little Cupid hearts. High school shit. Hell, it was more like grammar school shit. But it scared me nonetheless. How had I let myself fall so quickly, so completely, for this guy I had just met? A guy I really knew very little about. Maybe it was part of my genetics, passed down from my crazy mother.

Eventually, I thought about Kleinschmidt. He and

Malone were a package. I'd met them at the same time and my life changed dramatically. Before Malone entered my love life it had been a barren stretch on the road of romance for me.

The police still had no leads on Kleinschmidt's shooter. Malone said the file would remain open indefinitely, but without any viable information, there wasn't much hope of finding the guy responsible. Unless he tried the same stunt again with another cop and didn't get away so easily. It could happen.

When I finished my cider, I slipped off the pillows and went for a refill. I kept thinking about Malone's reaction to the baby book. It didn't take a detective to recognize how uncomfortable the subject made him. He wasn't too old to have kids—for that matter, neither was I. We hadn't been together that long and already I was doodling about marriage and Malone sounded ready to run.

Was I blowing this relationship too? Like every other one worth mentioning in the last ten years? Was this courtship doomed from the start? I resumed my perch and watched the snowflakes perform their gravitational dance.

Shortly after midnight the snow stopped. Everything outside my window appeared pure and freshly made. There were no wrappers stuck in the bushes, no cigarette butts or used condoms visible. Everything was brand new. A row of pine trees in the park across the street made me think of the holidays. Light from the street lamps and the stars above reflected in the white powder. There were no tire tracks or footprints to mar it. I was looking at a new creation, a world untouched by human hands. It was beautiful.

Malone would be here soon. Could I keep the relationship feeling brand new? Could I roll it in snow and keep it from falling apart? I didn't want to lose this guy, but I didn't know how not to drive him away. I felt like shit. My cider was gone. I fixed another one, put some Earl Klugh on the stereo and resumed my perch. The pillows were softer now, tempting me to stretch out. I did. Even the branches of the giant elms lining the street were thick with snow. Twinkles of reflected starlight reminded me of Malone's eyes.

"Jamie, open up." A steady tapping at my door woke me. I'd passed out on the pillows. My head throbbed as I tried to get up.

"Malone?" My mouth was full of fuzzy caterpillars.

"Yeah. You okay?" I fumbled the locks open and tugged on the door.

"Give me a minute or two. Gotta find my brain." I left him in the living room. In the bath, I splashed cold water on my face and drank half a cup of mouthwash.

He was sitting on the sofa when I came back. I flopped on the cushions, my head landing in his lap. He looked tired and more than a little concerned. Tenderly, he put his hand on my forehead.

"You okay, Jay?"

"Just a little bombed. Snow always gives me the blues. Guess I got loaded." I reached for the table and came up with the gift box. Somehow I managed to hand it to him. "Happy Thursday, Grover."

"What's this?" Malone turned the box over slowly, as if it might explode.

"I forget. Why don't you open it and find out." I tried to sit up twice but couldn't make it. So I gave up and stayed where I was.

He opened the box slowly, carefully slitting the tape with his thumb and sliding the paper out of the way. My eyes felt grainy and sore and it hurt to look through them, but I wanted to see his reaction as he opened my gift. It was worth the effort. He rewarded me with one of my favorite things, his low voltage smile. The one that made his eyes sparkle just a little, like the stars overhead in the winter sky.

"Well what do you know," Malone said softly.

"Nothing too extravagant. They work. I tried them

right away." My head was still banging, but I didn't care.

"Guess you're finally getting serious about locking the door." Malone gently ran his fingers through my hair. "Maybe you should go crawl into bed and sleep it off."

"Not unless you're going with me."

"Mind if I grab a shower? I feel like last year's sneakers."

"Help yourself. Just don't expect me to wash your back. I couldn't stand up without a harness and a safety net."

He kissed me gently and carried me into the bedroom. I had to fight the impulse to cling when Malone set me down. Here's a great way to improve your relationship. Greet your lover totally zonked on spiked cider while wearing a Chicago Bears sweatshirt and torn jeans. There wasn't enough ambition or coordination in me to even get out of my clothes. If I asked Malone to help, he might get the wrong idea.

The room wasn't exactly spinning, but it sure as hell wasn't holding still. I clung to a pillow, determined to wait for Malone to join me. Unfortunately, I passed out before the water started to run in the bath.

* * * *

Friday morning I felt a little better, but nowhere near human. Malone was still sleeping. I went to fix breakfast and surprise him for a change. Exhibiting the greatest degree of self-control, I didn't drink the coffee straight from the pot. I used a mug. For the second cup I added three scoops of sugar. Coffee, muffins and oranges were the best I could do. The food would eventually make me feel alive again. I was about to take Malone a tray when I noticed the bottle of Southern Comfort on the counter. Last night slowly swam back into focus. I'd cracked the seal on it when I made the first mug of cider. Now it was half empty. No wonder I had wiped out. I put the fifth away and turned to take Malone his meager breakfast. He

139

was standing behind me.

"Jesus, Angus, don't do that!"

He took the tray from my hands and set it on the table. Then he scooped me up for a kiss and carried me over to the Jewish Aunt. We snuggled. Every time I tried to talk, he silenced me with a kiss. Who can argue with that kind of reasoning? I took the hint. After a while Malone sat up and pulled me into his lap.

"We need to talk," he said softly.

"Yeah, I think so too."

"You want to go first?"

I shook my head. "I'll wait."

"There's something you should know, before we go any further. I'm an alcoholic. I haven't had a drink in over eight years. But I'm still an alcoholic. I should have told you before." He gave me a little squeeze around the shoulders. "Just never found the right moment."

I didn't know what to say. Quickly I thought about every time we'd been together. Malone drank coffee by the gallon and bottled water like a million other people, but I realized I'd never seen him with so much as a glass of wine. That one night after work, when I had converted the Dutch oven into a wine bucket, he hadn't even taken a sip. And I'd even washed both glasses.

"Why didn't you tell me, Angus? I feel like an idiot."

"Don't. You had no way of knowing. It doesn't bother me to see other people drink. I just take care of myself." He held me tenderly, stroking my back with his warm, strong hands.

"Booze is something I can live without. I don't need it." I couldn't tell if he believed me or not.

"I'll understand if you need some time to think, Jay. It's not like saying I used to go bowling. Alcoholism is a disease. It can be treated, but it needs attention every day."

I pulled away from him and got off the sofa. He didn't say anything while I walked around the room. I stopped before him, standing beyond his reach.

"How do you feel about me, Malone? Do you see me as something other than an easy piece of ass?"

His face flushed dark with anger. "You're a hell of a lot more than that."

I was frustrated, confused and afraid to say what was on my mind. But it came tumbling out just the same.

"We're not kids, Malone. Ever since I met you, there's been a very definite attraction here. Maybe it goes both ways." He started to speak but I waved his comment aside. "I think we have a shot at something good. What do you think?"

He didn't hesitate. "Same here."

"C'mere." I took his hand and led him into the kitchen. One of the cupboards above the stove serves as my liquor cabinet. It's not much. The Southern Comfort, a fifth of gin, tequila and the two bottles of wine I'd bought last night. I set each one on the counter with Malone at my elbow.

"Jay, this isn't necessary."

"Shut up, Angus, and start pouring." I unscrewed the gin and dumped the contents into the sink. He watched as the booze gurgled down the drain. I did the same to the tequila and the whiskey. Malone held back the wine.

"This is perfectly good wine. Don't pour it away, give it to a friend or take it back to the store. You're wasting money."

"Bullshit," I said angrily, "you mean more to me than some stupid bottle of wine. Give."

"Jamie, this is crazy."

"So have me committed." I snatched a bottle from him and fiddled with the wrapper, trying to get the cork out.

Malone gently but firmly took the bottle back. "You need a corkscrew." His voice softened to a whisper.

I dug one out of the drawer and handed it to him. Expertly, he sliced away the wrapper and twisted the opener, easing the cork out with a slight pop. He handed it back and I dumped it in the sink. By the time the first bottle was empty, the second one was ready. I ran the hot water through the pipes to flush the smell.

"There will be some happy sewer rats tonight." I turned away from the sink. Malone hugged me and began nibbling the soft spot on my neck, beneath my ear.

"Nicest thing anyone's ever done for me," he whispered.

"Come with me, big fella. We'll have to fix that."

CHAPTER THIRTEEN

Later, after a steamy shower, Malone helped me pack a big bag of clothes. He still wouldn't tell me where we were going. We swung by his place and loaded his Jeep with a suitcase and a duffel bag. Then we hit the road, headed north, away from the city. Last night's fluffy white snowstorm was reduced to mounds of ugly gray slush, heaped on the roadway by the early morning plows. So much for the image I'd had of a fresh new beginning. Malone drove along confidently, with the heater blasting and the stereo oozing Vivaldi's "Four Seasons". Between the morning's activities and last night's binge, I had a hard time keeping my eyes open. Sleep took me during "Spring".

It was late afternoon when we stopped and Malone nudged me awake. I let him prod me more than was necessary before opening my eyes. We were surrounded by snow. Not the dingy gray slop of the city, but tons of spun cotton candy. The Cherokee was parked beside an old Tyrolean inn, nestled in a hillside of pine trees. I expected to see strapping Austrian lads with flaxen hair and clear blue eyes, chopping wood and singing songs, but there was no one else in sight.

"Where the hell are we, Angus?"

"Boyne Falls. Why do I have the feeling you never get out of the city?" he teased.

"Because if I do, it's to go to another city." I rubbed my eyes. This had to be a dream. "What state are we in?"

He grinned. "Michigan, you dope. C'mon, let's go check in."

The desk clerk greeted Malone like an old friend, with a warm handshake and a quick pat on the back. He was a stocky man with a white goatee. The rest of his head was completely bald. Even his eyebrows were gone.

"David Erhardt, this is Jamie Richmond. She's a writer, so be careful what you say. It might end up in a book."

Erhardt swooped over and kissed my knuckles. Nobody ever kissed my hand in greeting before. My face flushed as he did it, and I shot Malone an evil look.

"It is a pleasure to make your acquaintance, my dear." Erhardt's voice had a lilting European accent. "Any friend of Malone's is an honored guest to my humble establishment. Should you desire anything during your stay it will be my esteem pleasure to assist you."

"Got my room ready, David?" Malone eased an arm around my waist and drew me back beside him. Suddenly he was being protective.

"Room? We have no mere rooms. We have suites!" Erhardt nearly spat in disgust at Malone's comment. "Holiday Inn has rooms."

"Pardon me all to hell. Is my *suite* ready?" Malone was obviously having a hard time keeping a straight face.

"Of course," Erhardt said. "We run a first-class establishment, even if the majority of our clientele are neophytes, such as you. Follow me."

Erhardt slid his arm through mine and escorted me to a wide-carpeted staircase. He didn't offer to help Malone with our bags, but gave us a running monologue on the origin of each piece of antique furniture we passed. He paused at the last door on the second floor and swung it open with a flourish. My chin dropped. Suite was an understatement. This was bigger than my apartment. There was a parlor decorated with Queen Anne reproductions, a fireplace and a pair of beveled glass French doors leading out to a balcony. Another set of doors led to the bedroom where a canopied king-size bed awaited my bones. The bathroom had no shower, but a large oval tub big enough for two. Brass fixtures were everywhere, tastefully appointed. The towels looked thicker than the carpeting in my apartment. I wanted to transport the whole room back to Plymouth. I wanted to move in here permanently.

"Does it meet with your approval?" Erhardt asked me.

"Bet your ass," Malone chuckled.

I ignored him. "It's beautiful, David."

Erhardt opened the doors to the balcony and waved me out beside him. Malone peered over my shoulder. The view overlooked a ski resort. I saw dozens of skiers in colorful outfits flash by as they schussed down the hill. With the white backdrop of the snow and the deep green tint of the pine trees, it was picturesque.

"Now if you will excuse me, I must see to the preparations for dinner." Erhardt pressed my hand and thumped Malone on the arm.

"What's on the menu?" Malone asked.

"We have several treats. The special is broiled elk tenderloin in a light cream sauce, with angel hair pasta and baby carrots. Perhaps escargot in puff pastry as an appetizer." David was ignoring Malone, considering my reaction. "Do you approve?"

"Sounds heavenly."

The bald head bobbed once. "Excellent. Dinner begins at seven. Enjoy." He slipped silently out the door.

We stood on the balcony for a while, surveying the slopes. Malone tugged me back inside and closed the doors. The frosted glass panels allowed us to view the scenery from the cozy comforts of the room.

"Do you like it?"

"I love it. But there's one problem, Angus."

He shook his head, the little smile playing on his lips. "Wrong again. What could possibly be a problem?"

"I don't know how to ski."

"You'll learn. We'll take lessons in the morning. Tonight we'll have a leisurely feast, then curl up in front of the fire and relax." He gestured toward the hearth. "You wanted a fireplace."

"How did you ever find this place?"

He led me to the couch, where we had the option of the view or the fire. "I came up here years ago to go skiing. Erhardt crashed into me on the slopes. To this day, I don't think it was an accident. David insisted on buying me dinner after knocking me down. At the time, he was the manager here. Now he owns it and a good chunk of other properties around the city."

"Dinner sounds like a four-star treat, Malone. Do you go to such lengths often?"

"I rarely eat more than two meals a day. Erhardt must be pulling out the stops for your sake. He lives to impress the ladies." His fingers were wandering through my hair.

"You are full of surprises, Angus."

"So are you, Jay."

* * * *

Saturday we spent on the ski slopes. Malone rented a set of equipment for me and accompanied me through a morning lesson, even though he's an experienced skier. I have to admit, I enjoyed it. Gliding over the powder in the fresh air is invigorating. The only move I could remember was the snowplow, where you point the tips of your skis together to stop. Just don't cross the tips, or you'll end up on your head. It took me a while to make it down the bunny hill, and I only fell twice. We had lunch in the ski lodge and planned the afternoon.

Malone was going to join me for another lesson, but I

knew it was boring for him. After assuring him I'd be fine on my own and we'd meet back at our suite when we were done, he set out for the advanced slopes. I went through another group lesson then took several trips up and down the bunny hills. There was a large crowd of skiers out and the majority of them did a good job keeping out of my way. I didn't even get frustrated at the nine-year-olds who were mastering the slopes with ease. I was having too much fun to worry about what other people thought of my own abilities.

I'd convinced myself to take one more run and was in line for the towrope when I saw her. We were at least fifty feet apart and the late afternoon sun was in my eyes, but I thought it was her. Clumsily, I skied out of line and worked my way toward the snack bar.

I'd swear it was Melissa Hatcher. She was wearing black ski pants and a gray down vest over a white turtleneck sweater. As I approached the lodge, a kid no older than five cut in front of me. It was either fall to the side or run the kid over. I fell. He fell too. By the time I got untangled and regained my feet, she was gone. Kicking off my skis, I ran into the snack bar looking for her. Vanished.

Maybe it hadn't been Melissa. Maybe it was someone who looked like her. After all, I'd only met her once. The slopes were jammed with young blonde snow bunnies.

My thighs ached and my buns were tired of kissing the ground. I returned my ski equipment and hiked along the path to Erhardt's. David met me at the door.

"You look absolutely radiant. I see the day on the slopes agreed with you." He was gushing with European charm.

I caught a glimpse of myself in the mirror beside the front desk. My face was bright red. My hair was matted to my skull. Every square inch of my clothing was dotted with snow.

"Right now I could use a hot shower and a masseuse."

147

I stamped the powder off my boots and shook out my hair.

"I would be more than happy to offer my massage talents, Jamie dear, but I do not believe Malone would appreciate it."

An idea hit me. "You've known Malone a long time, haven't you, David?"

"Many years." Erhardt made a little bow. "He is a good and generous friend, a fine man."

I waved away his compliments. "What's his first name?"

Erhardt looked confused. "His name is Malone. That is the only name I know."

I felt cheated. What did Malone have to hide? "But everyone has two names. What about his credit card?"

"Malone pays with cash. Even in the lean years, when there is no snow, Malone has always come to stay. Usually every other month, between November and April, he stays three nights at least, every time."

"I give up," I said with disgust.

David started walking me toward the suite. "You must be very special to Malone."

"Why do you say that?"

He smiled softly and raised his hands, palms up, in what must have been a European version of a shrug. "In all the years I have known Malone, you are the first woman he has ever brought here."

"You're kidding!"

"No, Jamie dear, I am quite serious." Erhardt pulled a passkey from his pocket and unlocked the door. "The very first."

"Almost like going home to meet his parents, huh?" I leaned against the wall and studied the innkeeper.

"Please, Jamie, do not misunderstand. I was merely making an observation."

"Thank you, David. Why do I get the feeling this is an elaborate practical joke?"

Erhardt shook his head. "There is a control panel in your suite, next to the bath. Try number three. I believe it is exactly what you need. Malone always skis until dark. Perhaps another hour before he will return."

Once in the room, I stripped off my wet jeans and the rest of my clothes. If Malone and I stayed together, I'd have to get some real ski duds. I filled the tub with the hottest water I could stand and bent over the control panel. Button number three activated a hidden whirlpool system. Gingerly, I lowered my body into the tub and let the heat relax me. I didn't get out until half an hour later, when the water finally turned cold. Malone still wasn't back.

I dressed for dinner in a black leather skirt and wool sweater, and went to wait for Malone on the balcony. Evening darkness filled the valley as I gazed out toward the slopes. I noticed a trail leading from the Inn toward the direction of the ski lodge. At the edge of that path, I caught a glimpse of someone. Malone was wearing a Kelly green outfit with a white stripe down the side. I thought I saw him enter the path, skis jauntily bouncing on his shoulders. Near an overhang of trees, I saw a figure stop and converse with him.

The distance was too great for me to get a good look at either of them. With the sun gone, I wasn't even positive it was Malone. The sky was black. The nearest streetlight was in Detroit. It was getting too cold to hang around the balcony, so I stepped inside the French doors and warmed my buns by the fire. I could still look out the window and see most of the path. The two people continued their discussion. The one without the skis kept gesturing wildly with his arms, and the other one nodded enthusiastically. I sat by the fire to wait. A few minutes later my phone rang.

"Hey, Jay," Malone said warmly in my ear.

"Where are you?"

"Making arrangements for tomorrow. The slopes are jammed on Sundays. I've got some other plans in mind."

"What's the matter, Claude? Afraid I'll wipe out a bunch of Sunday school kids on the bunny hill?"

"It crossed my mind," he was chuckling softly. "Tell David to send up some hot appetizers to hold us until dinner. I'll be there in ten minutes, but I want to clean up."

"You owe me a thorough body massage to recover from the lumps I took today. I'm not used to all this healthy exercise."

"I'll see what I can do. Bye, Jay."

"Bye, Claude."

I jiggled the hook and got the front desk, relaying Malone's request. He came through the door with the room service waiter, who placed the tray on a low table before the fire and bowed silently out of the room. Malone gave me a frozen kiss and popped the lid off the tray.

"What the hell is that?" I asked.

A circular loaf of dark bread rested in the center of the tray. The top of the loaf had been cut into sections, like wedges from a pie. Malone pried one up and bent closer to the bread, sniffing. When he looked up, I caught one of those killer low voltage smiles. It made my spine tingle.

"Well?"

"It's shepherd's bread. Knowing Erhardt, it's probably filled with cheese and some kind of sauce." He dipped the edge of the bread into the goo and extended it toward me. Now I could smell it. I tested the sample.

"What do you think?" Malone was waiting for my reaction, another wedge of bread dangling from his fingers.

"If Erhardt made this himself, you might be replaced before morning."

Malone sat on the floor and scooped some onto a plate for me. We didn't talk much while we devoured the appetizer. Malone nodded, admiring my outfit.

"Give me a minute to get cleaned up, and we'll go down for dinner." He struggled off the floor and headed for the bedroom.

"What about my rubdown?"

"Patience, Jamie, patience."

Dinner was suitable for a state dinner. Erhardt's dining room was small, with room for only forty people at discreetly positioned tables. A harpist played softly in the corner by the door and all conversations were muted and refined. I felt like royalty. We dined on Wisconsin cheese soup. Broiled scallops with lemon butter and triple chocolate torte for dessert. Plus enough freshly baked bread to add two inches to my hips.

After dinner we got our coats and took a walk through the streets. Music blared from the bars and cafes, audible through the doors. A number of shops displayed handmade crafts and collectibles. Malone left me outside a health food store and came back with a small package and a goofy grin. We held hands and wandered about. I liked it. Boyne Falls is a long way from Detroit, in more ways than one. I've been a big city girl all my life, silently scoffing at any metropolitan area smaller than five hundred thousand people. But I could get used to small town living.

Back at the inn, Malone made me wait by the fire for a minute. He came back with the top sheet from the bed and spread it on the carpet.

"You can't be serious," I giggled.

"I promised you a rubdown. And I try to always keep my promises." He turned me around and slowly undressed me, folding my clothes over the back of the sofa. Shyly, I slid to my knees, and lay down on the sheet.

"Be gentle with me, Claude. I've had an exhausting day," I mumbled.

Malone let out a low whistle. "That's an understatement. You've got a bruise back here the size of Montana." He fingered a spot on my right hip.

"That must be where the kid knocked me down."

He removed a bottle of avocado oil he'd bought at the health food store and began working it into my flesh. My weary muscles began to relax as he kneaded them. My god, he had strong hands. As he worked, I let my mind wander, seeing the girl who looked like Melissa Hatcher. Lately, I hadn't given her much thought. But it seemed like Kleinschmidt was never far from my mind. Malone rolled me over and began massaging the tendons in my ankles and the arches of my feet.

"Where'd you learn how to do that?"

"Self-taught with years of practice." His voice was soft and deep, just the way I like it. I tried to see his eyes, but they were cast down, focused on my feet.

"You certainly know how to rub a woman the right way," I groaned.

"It's all in the wrists." Malone worked his way up to my calves. Somehow, the massage was relaxing and erotic at the same time.

"Wish I could stop thinking about Kleinschmidt," I mumbled with my eyes closed.

Malone rocked back on his heels, pulling his hands off my legs. I waited for the rubdown to continue. When it didn't, I opened my eyes. I had to prop up on my elbows in order to see him. There was a dark, disgusted look on his face.

"You're impossible. I'm trying to relax you and treat you to a romantic weekend and all you want to do is talk about Kleinschmidt. What's the matter with you?" Malone got to his feet, rubbing his slippery hands on a towel. "I give up, Jamie."

"Hey, Claude."

He ignored me and went to the window. I scrambled to my feet and came to stand beside him. Large overhead lights illuminated a few of the slopes near the lodge. Hundreds of people were playing follow the leader down the hill. From here it looked like a gigantic neon snake as the lights reflected off the various colored outfits. It looked like fun.

Malone pulled away when I touched his shoulder. I slugged it until he faced me.

"Don't tune me out, Malone," I snapped angrily.

He grabbed me by the shoulders. It was cool over here by the window and I was still naked. I wanted to be back by the fire, cozying up with him. Why was he suddenly being so crazy about this?

"Let it go, Jamie. You're obsessed with Kleinschmidt and the shooting. I don't know if I can keep hanging around if you don't stop." His eyes were darkly serious.

"I'm sorry, Malone. Sometimes when I get caught up in a problem, I have a hard time not thinking about it."

He drew me to his chest, pinning my arms against my sides. "Let it go."

How could I refuse him? Besides, he was right. I was haunted by something I could do nothing about. It was like trying to fly because I was holding a chicken wing in each hand. It made no sense at all. "Okay, I'll forget it ever happened. Except for one very important thing."

He loosened his grip until we could see eye to eye. "What's that?"

"If it wasn't for that night, would I have ever met you?"

He smiled a thin one. "Good point. Just forget about the bad stuff with Kleinschmidt."

"Who?"

"That's more like it." He reached down and patted my bottom. "Your ass is freezing."

"Maybe you'd better help me warm it."

CHAPTER FOURTEEN

Sunday morning we had a sunrise feast in bed. Erhardt sent up platters of mushroom crepes, sausages, pastries and fresh fruit salad, along with a gigantic pot of coffee. I could have spent the day in bed without a complaint. After breakfast, we soaked in a bubble bath, splashing suds almost to the ceiling. I'd never made love in a bath before. Things certainly got very slippery. When we came out, Malone had another surprise for me. Waiting on the bed was a quilted nylon suit, heavy woolen socks and a pair of thick boots with rubber soles.

"What is this for?"

"Today's outdoor activity. Wear a sweater and some jeans underneath and you'll be comfortable." Malone was already dressing in a similar outfit.

"Wait a minute, Hugo. What is it exactly that we're going to do?" The image of curling up in bed for the day was still fresh in my brain.

"Get dressed," he said stubbornly. That's just what this relationship needs, two stubborn halves. I did what he asked, albeit slowly. Malone was sitting on the edge of the bed, impatiently drumming his fingers on his knees.

"You got rhythm," I muttered.

"I should have got you up an hour earlier. It'll be noon before we leave the room."

I turned to face him, half of my upper lip tinted with gloss. "If you had gotten me up an hour earlier, I'd still be in bed. The patient man is greatly rewarded."

Malone shrugged, frowned, and went down to the lobby to bullshit with Erhardt. I took my time. If I hurried now, he'd begin to expect it all the time. No sense getting his hopes up. They were arguing about football when I joined them.

"Ravishing!" David Erhardt exclaimed, blowing me a kiss with his fingertips.

"About time," Malone grunted playfully.

I struck a model's pose at the base of the stairs and looked haughtily over my shoulder. Both men laughed.

"Now will you please tell me what the hell we're going to do?"

Malone shook his head. "Nope, but I will show you." He slapped David on the shoulder and led me outside.

Waiting in the snow beside Malone's truck were two small snowmobiles. They looked brand new, glistening with moisture on the hoods. Malone dug some keys out of his pocket and started each unit up.

"I've never done this before, Hugo," I yelled over the noise.

"That's what you said about skiing. Look how quickly you picked that up. This is easier. Right hand throttle, left hand brake. You steer by turning the handle bars." Malone grinned as he strapped on his crash helmet.

"This is crazy, Hugo!"

"Trust me, Jay. You'll love it. I've seen you drive; this is right up your alley." With that he unceremoniously crammed a matching helmet over my head. Malone had thought of everything. Malone sat me on the sled and showed me the basics in a thirty-second crash course. I wished he hadn't referred to it in those terms.

"Just follow me. We're going on a regular trail, part of

the state forest. It's well maintained. We'll be traveling about an hour before we stop." Then he gently worked the safety strap for the helmet under my chin and tightened it.

"What if I have to pee?"

"You should have thought of that before you got dressed. Let's ride."

"I hate you, Hugo," I muttered inside my helmet. Malone moved easily to his sled and climbed aboard. He waved at me then put the machine in gear. Reluctantly, I followed. We cut away from the lodge and the ski slopes and worked our way deeper into the woods that surrounded the area.

I would never admit it to Malone, but he had been right. I did love it. The snowmobile reminded me of a motorcycle, which I'd always enjoyed riding. The scenery was incredible. We moved through some of the most breathtaking forests I'd ever seen. Evergreen skyscrapers towered above us, clutching bits of snow to their boughs. The trail weaved back and forth, avoiding any clusters of trees too dense to ride through. Malone would slow down and glance back occasionally just to make sure I hadn't missed a turn and burst into a fireball. He was probably more concerned about the trees than he was about me. What's worse, the bum lied to me. It was two hours before he stopped, pulling his machine off the trail beside an old gravel pit. Malone switched off his snowmobile and waved me up alongside him.

"Well?" He worked his helmet off and set it on the seat behind him.

"Well what?" I yawned and popped my ears. The sudden silence took a little getting used to. My head felt sweaty as I yanked the helmet off. I looked away from his grinning face, hiding my own smile.

"You're a lousy liar, Jay," he said with a chuckle.

"Yeah, well you can't tell time for shit, Hugo. I almost peed my pants half-an-hour ago."

As I turned to look at him, I was pelted in the face with

a snowball. If that wasn't bad enough, he jumped off his sled and tackled me. We ended rolling around in a drift, throwing handfuls of powder at each other. I managed to get a fair amount down the collar of his suit, where I'm sure it melted on his back. We were both laughing when Malone sat up, and silently pointed below us. During our harmless playing, we had rolled dangerously close to the edge of the pit. It was packed with snow. Some of the drifts were probably eight feet deep, while other spots had less than an inch. By my estimation, it was at least ninety feet from the ledge where we sat to the bottom of the bowl. This was not my idea of a scenic rest stop. No restrooms or hot cocoa.

"Look over there," Malone said quietly.

Not thirty feet away from where we sat was a small wooded area. Standing perfectly still just beyond the trees were three deer. I'm no expert, but I think it was a mother and two fawns. I know there are occasional sightings of animals back in the city, but I've never seen them up close before.

"They're beautiful," I whispered.

We sat there silently for several minutes until the mother decided it was time to go. Gracefully she walked back into the woods, the two fawns automatically following her lead.

"Hey, check it out," Malone said, pointing toward the base of the gravel pit.

I followed his finger but couldn't see anything significant. "Yippee. More snow. When I get home, I'm moving to Arizona," I teased. "The only snow I want to see will be in a paper cone with raspberry syrup."

"See the tracks. People have been riding down there."

If I squinted I could make them out in the distance. "Isn't this state land?" I asked.

"Nah, we left the state forest about a mile back. This is private property. It's closed during the winter. But some of the woods, like where the deer were, wraps around the land. I'm sure the deer live deeper in the woods."

I looked down into the pit again. The sides were steep and scarred no doubt from years of excavation. I wondered if this was a working site. As I studied the formation, the ground beneath me shifted. I was turning to face Malone when the snow gave way and I went sliding down into the bowl.

"Shit! Shit! Shit!" I kept screaming as I fell down the wall, rushing toward who knew what at the base. The suit did a good job of protecting me, but it was a long way from a comfortable ride.

Years ago, I'd dated a macho man who insisted we go white water rafting. Suicidal water sports rank right up there beside cannibalism in my book. But he was persistent and the only guy I'd dated in a while, so I grudgingly went along. One of the things the guide warned us about was falling out of the raft. Once you're out, you're out. There would be no climbing back in. This wasn't like a horse that you could turn around anywhere and reverse your trail. The current was running fast and furious, and there wasn't much hope of stopping the ten-man raft and paddling back upstream to pick up the hapless passenger.

What the guide instructed us to do was, if you fall in, lie on your back, point your feet downstream, wrap your arms across your chest and hang on. When the current slows, make for the shore. Sooner or later, someone would be along for you. Of course, one hour after we entered the rapids, I went over the side. It was at least two hours before anyone came looking for me. Macho man made the rest of the trip with two blonde chicks from Calgary who liked to share. We broke up that night.

Now, as I was shooting down the wall of the gravel pit, I remembered the guide's instructions. The nylon suit hindered the process of wrapping my arms, but the extra padding helped. I pointed my feet at the bottom, closed my eyes and screamed all the way. Where the hell was my helmet when I needed it?

When I got near the bottom, my right ankle caught a boulder that was frozen in place. Despite the heavy padding of the boots, a jolt of pain ripped through me. I rebounded off the rock and went spinning sideways down the last forty feet of pit. At one point I was going headfirst at a pile of rocks. I could envision my skull, crushing like a ripe melon as it rammed into the stones. Somehow I twisted around in time. I took the rocks against my left side and bounced past the outcropping, sliding the rest of the way into the base of the pit.

Numerous curses rolled from my lips as I lay on the ground. My head was spinning so badly I couldn't tell which direction was up. My eyes refused to focus on anything. The remains of breakfast began to rise from my stomach, but I managed to choke them back down.

"Malone! Where the hell are you?" My ears were buzzing and I could hear my own heartbeat thumping in my head. I was alive, but by how much and for how long? Didn't people die from exposure?

What had happened to Malone? Had he tried to grab me before I'd gone over the edge, his hands slipping across the slick nylon suit, unable to find a purchase for his fingers? Had...had he pushed me? Was this some sick, sadistic game? Lull Jamie into a romantic stupor then shove her narrow ass over the edge of a cliff? Even if she did survive the ride down, could she find her way out before hypothermia set in? What about food and water?

"Malone, where are you?" My voice didn't work above a whisper. I still couldn't focus my eyes and my head felt like it was stuffed with cotton. "I promise I'll never call you funny names again. Help me."

The buzzing in my head grew louder, until I succumbed to the noise.

* * * *

It was a beautiful dream. I was lying on the sand,

feeling the warmth of the sun on my face. I was wearing my favorite bikini, the black one with the gold stripes on the hips. Nearby was a cabana with tropical drinks, complete with those silly little umbrellas. I was golden brown, even where the suit covered me. Paradise. Suddenly a large shadow fell across me. I looked up to see who dared interfere with my tan.

Malone. But it was not the passionate, charismatic man who had so easily swept me off my feet. No champion of kisses, no breakfast in bed. No romantic dinners, with soft music, candles and caresses. This was a sinister Malone, with no twinkle in the eyes, no soft voice to unhinge my knees. Was this the real Malone?

"You should have left it alone." His voice had a funny, metallic tone to it. As I raised my arm to hide my eyes, he began to stab me in the side with an enormous knife. I screamed and Malone let loose a hideous laugh. With each thrust of the blade, he mockingly called my name. His voice grew louder until he was shouting. "Jamie, Jamie, Jamie..."

"Jamie, c'mon baby, talk to me," Malone said.

I opened my eyes and screamed. "Get away from me!" Somehow I scrambled backwards, driving myself away from him. My chest was pounding with the urgency of my heart. I stopped when Malone didn't try to follow, only knelt there looking at me like I was a lunatic. I tried to sit up, but couldn't make it.

I looked down. This wasn't a sandy beach. It was a snow covered mess. Rocks jutted out of the snow haphazardly. I had the impression of empty beer bottles floating out with the tide, only to come to rest somewhere on the other side of the world. In the distance, I heard Malone call out.

"Take it easy, baby. That was some ride you took." Malone came toward me slowly. Behind him I could see the snowmobile he'd been riding.

"What happened, Hugo?" There went my pain-induced

promise. It hurt my side to talk.

"You went sliding off the edge like a penguin. The snow beneath you must have given way. I turned around to check the machines, make sure they weren't too close. I looked back and you were gone. Are you all right, Jay?"

"I don't know, Malone. Every inch of my body hurts." I tried not to cringe as he knelt beside me again.

"Anywhere hurt more than the rest?" His voice was gentle and caring. Even his eyes showed concern.

"Ribs," I pointed with my left hand.

Tenderly he unzipped the nylon suit enough so he could reach his hand inside. When he put pressure on my ribs, a scream escaped my lips.

"Probably broke one," Malone said softly, "where else?"

I couldn't breathe now and talking was out of the question. I didn't want him to touch me if it was going to hurt anymore. I pointed at my head and my right foot. I held my breath, waiting for him to start probing at one end or the other. Nothing happened.

"If you rapped your skull hard enough, you might have a concussion." Malone's voice was soothing. "If your foot or ankle's broken, taking your boot off is the worst thing to do. We're a long way from civilization."

He ran a bare hand across my face, wiping away the excess snow. Gently he raked the hair out of my eyes. Was this for real, or was I just imagining it?

"What are we going to do, Malone?" I managed to whisper.

"We need to get you to a hospital, Jay, or at the very least, a doctor."

"They must have emergency medical services out here in God's country. Go drop a dime on 911."

He managed a tiny trace of a smile. "Not the way you're thinking. I already checked, there's no cellular service available. The nearest town is about ten miles away. I don't want to leave you here alone, but I don't think you can handle the ride on a sled."

"I'll make it." I tried to sit up and fell back.

Malone's hands squeezed mine. "Lie still a minute. Let me take a look around."

He left me lying there in the snow. I had no way of tracking the time. The longer I lay there, the more I ached. What I wouldn't give for a whirlpool and a massage right now. I must have drifted off again, because I didn't even hear the snowmobile start up when he moved it. Only when he picked me up did the pain bring me around.

"Ow! Jesus Christ, Malone! You're going to pay for this."

"Nice to have you back among the living, Jay." He tried to sound relaxed, but his eyes gave him away. They weren't smiling as he lowered me down.

"What's the plan, Hugo?" I had to grind my teeth together to keep from screaming. Damn, it hurt to move.

"There's a house about a mile or so back up the road. We're going to try for that. I don't want to bounce you around too much, so we'll go slowly. If you've broken a rib, it might puncture your lung if we're not careful."

"Now there's an image I could do without. Do you have any encouraging words?"

He wasn't talking anymore. Maybe he was afraid to say something. As long as he was taking me with him, I felt reasonably safe. For the time being, that was. Keeping my mouth shut is hard for me, but I did it anyway. It was the only way to hold the screams inside. Because if I let them out, there would be another question that needed answering—would they be screams of pain or fear?

Malone settled me down on top of some pine branches. Everything smelled like a Christmas tree. He piled more branches around me then walked away. I couldn't lie completely down, but I could curl up and get reasonably comfortable. I heard the machine start up, and felt us begin to move. My head didn't like the idea. I closed my eyes and blacked out again.

* * * *

I awoke in a hospital bed. Clean starched sheets rubbed against my tender skin. Faded white walls devoid of any artwork stared back at me. My vision was clear. My ears were no longer ringing. There was a dull ache in the back of my skull, no worse than Friday morning after my tango with Southern Comfort. A single intravenous needle was taped to the back of my left hand. Hanging over the rail by my right hand was a nurse's call button. I thumbed it.

A skinny girl no older than twenty appeared in the doorway. Long black hair woven into a braid trailed down her back. If she wore a nametag, it was hidden beneath her cardigan sweater. She checked my pulse and temperature before speaking.

"How are you feeling?"

"Like I played chicken with a runaway freight train and lost."

"What's your name?"

Obviously she planned on testing my mental capacities. Malone would have filled in any necessary paperwork. "Jamie Rae Richmond. I live in Plymouth."

She nodded. "Good." One hand rose before my face. "How many fingers?"

I groaned. "Two. Thumb and pinkie, Texas Longhorn style. Satisfied?"

"Yes. Are you hungry?"

"No." My stomach revolted at even the suggestion of eating. "Where's Malone?"

She smiled. "Is he that great-looking guy with the blue eyes?"

"That's him."

She sighed and smoothed out the blankets. "He's in the lobby."

"Send him in?"

"Sure thing." She wiggled out the door and started to

pull it shut behind her. Malone didn't wait for an invitation. He barged right on in.

"Hey, Jay."

"Hey, Malone. What's going on?"

"You've been out a long time." He looked a lot more relieved than the last time I saw him.

I found the controls for the hospital bed and managed to elevate my head. There's no fun in lying down alone. "So how bad is it?"

He smiled one of his best low wattage numbers. "You've a broken right ankle, two, count 'em, two broken ribs and a slight concussion. The doctors suggest an overnight stay, then release in the morning if everything goes well."

"Aw shit, Malone. I ruined your weekend."

"Forget it, Jay. There will be plenty of other weekends."

"How did you get me out of the pit, Hugo? I don't remember a thing, other than riding along in a Christmas tree."

Malone nodded. "Those were branches from a pine to soften the ride. You were in the bucket from an old farm tractor. I found it with some other equipment not too far from where you landed. I rigged a towrope behind my sled and dragged it along. It worked pretty well for the short ride."

"How'd we get here?" I had trouble talking without yawning.

"We made it to that farmhouse, about a mile from the pit. Turns out the guy who lives there is a volunteer fireman. He ran for the ambulance and drove us in." He slid a hip onto the bed and rested one hand on mine. "When they were sure you were okay, he took me back to pick up the other sled. The rental place is sending a trailer out to haul them back."

"What about you? How are you going to get back to Erhardt's inn?"

"I'm staying with you."

I was touched. He really meant to spend the night in a wooden armchair, watching over me. With my free hand, I reached up and squeezed his.

"That's sweet, Hugo. But it's not necessary. Go back to the inn, have a delicious meal and get a good night's sleep. Maybe you can even get in some skiing in the morning, before they cut me loose."

"I don't know, Jamie. . ."

"Look, Malone, this is your holiday weekend. I'm not going to do anything but sleep until morning anyway. There's no need for you to baby-sit me. I'm a big girl." If he wanted to fawn over me, I'd prefer it be at home.

He bent down and kissed me, cool lips on my face. "As long as you're sure you'll be okay," he said.

"I'm positive. Go have a sinful dinner and swap lies with Erhardt. Who knows what time the doc will cut me loose tomorrow? You might as well enjoy the skiing while you can."

His eyes sparkled with a smile. "Get some rest, Jay. I'll see you in the morning. Just call the inn and I'll be here before you know it."

"Good night, Hugo." I wiggled my fingers at him as he left the room.

In a way, I didn't want him to leave. But for some reason his presence made me uncomfortable. My thoughts were still jumbled, no doubt from my noggin getting bounced around like a basketball at a Pistons -- Bulls game. I needed time to get all the pieces back where they belonged. I couldn't contemplate things rationally with Malone pressing my hand. After a while I gave up and sleep overtook me.

CHAPTER FIFTEEN

Just before dawn, one dream kept replaying on the movie screen of my mind. I was sitting on the rim of the gravel pit, staring down at the drifts of snow. Malone came up behind me and gave me a solid push. My head was turning back to look at him and the eyes that had successfully seduced me so many times were cold black orbs, empty of emotions. They were the eyes of a killer.

I woke up trembling and gasping for breath. A nurse stood beside my bed, talking quietly to me. She disconnected the intravenous bag from my arm and helped me sit up. A breakfast tray arrived with cold runny eggs and limp bacon. I pushed it away and opted for the toast and tea.

Was my imagination playing tricks on me? Or had Malone really pushed me? If so, why? Had he done it as a joke, playfully trying to knock me into the snow? Or was there a more serious, sinister reason? What did I really know about Malone anyway? He wouldn't do anything to hurt me, would he? No, not after the last few weeks. But how much can you trust a guy with only one name?

"You're imagining things!" I mumbled loudly to myself. Malone was the best thing to happen to me in years. Hell, he was the best thing ever! My cynical imagination was twisting him into a sadistic ghoul. Christ, no wonder I can't keep a relationship going. I could hear my mother whispering the same thought at me. *You'll never be happy with a man if you constantly keep magnifying his faults.* Just the type of motherly advice you'd expect from a woman with more failed relationships than the Detroit Lions have had winning seasons.

I finished breakfast about the same time the doctor came in to check me over. My head was clear, my vision back to normal. Gingerly he probed my skull, trying to find any soft spots. He showed me how to adjust the rib belt and recommended I see my own doctor as soon as I got home. I called Malone at the inn, to tell him I was free. At least, I would be, as soon as he arrived. David Erhardt came on the line.

"Jamie, dear, how goes the recovery?"

"Fine, David. The doc said I could be released. Can you tell Malone to come pick me up?'

"Ah, Malone is on the slopes. He hoped to get a few runs in before leaving tomorrow. Would you mind if I called for you?"

"I don't want to impose, David."

I could imagine Erhardt's hands waving away the comment as he spoke. "It is no imposition, dear. You are a guest at my hotel. Actually the majority of my patrons left last night to return to their hectic city lives. I shall not take no for an answer. I'll be along shortly."

"Thank you, David," I said meekly.

I swung my legs off the bed and studied my body through the hospital gown. A lumpy cast covered my right ankle and most of my foot. My ribs didn't hurt too badly, if I moved slowly. I called the nurse and asked her about my clothes. She brought a plastic bag with my jeans and the sweater I'd been wearing yesterday. With her help, I was able to get the sweater over my head. I didn't think there was any way those jeans would make it over my ankle.

"Are these comfortable?" the nurse asked.

"Yeah, they are one of my favorite pairs. How do I get them on?"

"We could cut them at the seam with a scalpel, just high enough to slide over the cast. Then we can tape them together."

I nodded. "What the hell."

She came back with my altered jeans and helped me into them. A couple of wide strips of surgical tape held the cloth together. David arrived as I was taking a trial run down the corridor with a set of wooden crutches. The bulk of the cast forced me to lean on my left foot to compensate, making me move like a drunk. David smiled and rubbed his goatee thoughtfully while I approached.

"Perhaps I could interest you in one of my legendary massages." Erhardt bowed and made a sweeping gesture with his hand.

"You gonna help me out of here or do I walk back to your hotel?" I wobbled crazily on the crutches and almost lost my balance.

"I am your chauffeur. Walk this way." David turned and strolled toward the door.

"If I could walk that way, I wouldn't need crutches or a chauffeur," I muttered.

Erhardt got me back to the inn and inside the lobby. I stopped to rest on a velvet armchair. My armpits were already turning raw from the handles of the crutches. David took them from me and propped them behind the registration desk.

"What would you like? Brunch? Perhaps some herbal tea?"

I shook my head. "I'm not hungry. But I'd kill for a hot bath."

He smiled widely. "No need to go to such lengths. A bath you want, a bath you shall have."

David Erhardt plucked me off the chair as if I were a

rag doll and carted me up the stairs. He didn't break a sweat by the time he got me to our room. I was impressed. Erhardt is a good three inches shorter than Malone. He didn't strike me as the physical type. Maybe there was more to be said for living in the wilderness. He carried me into the bath, and eased me down on the lid of the toilet.

"Don't think I can handle this with my foot wrapped in plaster," I said, looking longingly at the tub.

"We northern types are quite resourceful." David spun the dials on the tub and began filling it with steaming hot water. Then he opened the cupboard beneath the sink and removed a large plastic bag and a roll of duct tape. "Surely my dear, you do not believe that you are the first guest to ever break a bone skiing. Our suites are all stocked with the proper equipment."

He slipped the plastic over my cast and strapped it securely with the tape. When the tub was full, he closed the pipe and stepped back. I was still wearing my sweater and jeans and he'd made no attempt to help me remove them.

"Yvonne will be up in a moment to assist you. She will also return to help you out of the tub. Malone is due back at noon. I have sent word to the ski lodge, informing him of your arrival."

"You're very considerate, David. Thank you for everything."

"All part of the service. I'll send Yvonne along." He gave me one of his little bows and ducked out of the room. I managed to get my sweater off and unhook my jeans before I heard a gentle tap at the door. In came a big round woman, wearing a loose white jacket and black and white checked pants. She had large rosy cheeks and a wide friendly smile. Strands of silver gray hair were tucked under a bright blue bandana.

"Mr. Erhardt asked me to help you. I'm afraid there are no other women on duty today." Her voice was loud and friendly, with a hint of laughter.

"Thanks. I could use a hand."

Yvonne's smile grew. "More likely you could use a leg. Let's get those things off and get you in."

When I was naked, she steadied me long enough to help me into the tub. The water felt heavenly on my sore body. Without asking, Yvonne turned on the whirlpool system and nodded as I slouched down into the streams.

"I will be back shortly. I have a cake in the oven that needs my attention. If I leave it to Mr. Erhardt, it will end up in the garbage." Yvonne waved as she closed the bathroom door.

I lathered up with the scented bar of soap and began to relax as the heat soaked away my aches. My mind went back to the strange dream I had this morning, with Malone deliberately knocking me off the edge of the gravel pit. It just didn't make any sense. Why would he want to hurt me?

Maybe whatever painkillers they had given me had caused these silly thoughts. Malone wouldn't hurt me.

Would he?

* * * *

Something was very wrong! The water around me was ice cold and pulling me deeper. I opened my eyes and saw Malone kneeling beside the tub, dressed in his ski outfit. His arms were stuck into the water and his hands were clutching my shoulders. He was forcing me under.

I struggled against him and tried to push off the bottom of the tub, but he was too strong for me. If only I could break the surface of the water, I could breathe. I twisted and bucked against him, feeling the fire at my side as my ribs turned in protest.

Suddenly he pulled and yanked my head out of the water. Gagging and gasping, I drew in deep gulps of sweet air. The pain in my ribs subsided. Malone held me, one arm around my back for support.

"Christ, Jamie that was a stupid thing to do!"

"You tried to drown me, Malone!" I wanted to push him away but didn't have the strength.

"What? I came in and you were barely breathing. I thought you were dead! You must have fallen asleep and slipped under." He pulled one of the thick towels off the rack and wiped my face. I noticed his hands were shaking. Malone reached over and opened the drain, then lifted me out of the tub.

"I can get out by myself!" I was getting tired of being treated like an invalid.

"Yeah, just like you can take a bath by yourself," Malone said angrily. "You almost drowned. You should know better than to do a fool stunt like that."

"Shut up, Malone!" I slapped his face, hard.

"Hey, what the-"

"Stop treating me like some stupid kid." I was mad now, no longer frightened.

"Hey, let's talk about this," Malone said, stepping away from me.

I rocked back on the cast and sat slowly on the toilet seat. "Leave me alone. Just leave me the fuck alone!"

"Okay. You got it." He left the bathroom and shut the door behind him.

I used another towel to dry off and give myself something to do. Subconsciously, I reached into the tub and felt the last of the cold water as it was flowing down the drain. There was a gentle rap at the door.

"Go to hell!" I snapped.

"It's Yvonne. Can I help?"

I felt stupid. "Sure, come in."

The smile was gone from her face as she peeked around the edge of the door. "I am so sorry I didn't come back as soon as I should have. Mr. Erhardt had a few people arrive for luncheon, and I am the only cook on duty until this evening."

The image of Malone hovering above the tub remained

before my eyes. "How long has it been since you left, Yvonne?"

"About an hour, Miss. I am very sorry. Can I help you with anything?" Her face showed no trace of the humor I'd seen earlier. She undid the tape and removed the plastic wrapper from my cast.

"Sure. Give me a hand getting into the bedroom. I've got some clean things in there." I gave her the best smile I could muster.

She brightened visibly. "Of course." Firmly she slipped a big arm around my waist and helped me stump my way to the bed. I fished a clean pair of panties out of my suitcase, and a camisole. Yvonne helped me put the rib belt back in place then slip the camisole and a heavy woolen sweater over my head. The jeans were the same ones I'd worn earlier. I felt better when I was dressed. Yvonne relaxed and went back to her kitchen. Malone came in with my crutches and leaned against the wall.

"Hey, Jay."

"Hey, Malone."

"You okay?"

"I'm better. Sorry if I was acting like such a shit. Must have been some residual effect from the painkillers they gave me. What happened?"

He shrugged. "I came back when I got David's message. When I went into the bath, you were floating below the surface. I grabbed you and tried to bring you around, but you kept fighting me. For a while there, I thought I'd lost you."

"I must have passed out. When I came to, you were standing above me, with your hands on my neck. I thought you were trying to hold me under."

"That's crazy, Jamie!" His face went red with anger.

"I know," I muttered, unable to look at him anymore.

Malone walked over and knelt before me. "Why don't we get out of here? We could head back to the city and be there in time for dinner."

"I thought you wanted to stay tonight? We could travel tomorrow morning."

Malone shook his head. "This weekend hasn't been exactly what I planned. Let's go home. You'll feel more comfortable in your own place."

I nodded. It didn't take much to convince me. As much as I liked Erhardt's Inn, nothing sounded as safe right now as being in my own home.

We got back to my apartment around seven Monday night and Malone helped me get settled in. He ran around the corner to the Korean Garden restaurant and brought back enough food for ten people. We ate everything. I moved to the Jewish Aunt and managed to prop my cast on the coffee table. By hugging the arm of the sofa, I was able to stay upright. Malone sat beside me.

"Hey, Jay," he said softly.

"Hey, Malone." I turned my head to look at him closely. There was a quality in his eyes I'd never seen before. It took me a moment to realize it was sadness.

"You don't really think I could do anything to hurt you, do you, Jamie?"

"No. But you have to admit, it was a pretty painful weekend for me." I saw his eyes soften. It made me feel better. But there was still a dark corner in my mind where doubt was jumping up and down, crying out for attention. Sometimes you have to ignore those signals. This was one of those times.

"But there were some good points, weren't there?"

I nodded. "Yeah, skiing was fun. And I was enjoying the snowmobiles. Next time, we'll stay away from the gravel pits."

He leaned close and kissed the bottom of my ear. "What about the room? And the meals? And the fireplace? And the massage?" he whispered.

"Okay, that was good too." Doubt's corner began to grow dimmer. "I guess the weekend wasn't a total loss."

"Glad to hear it." His lips moved around and found

mine. They were soft and warm, almost melting. When he kissed me like that, it became difficult to determine where Malone ended and I began. We just blended into each other. "Want me to split so you can get some rest?" he whispered.

Any possible reservations I had about him were vanishing fast. There was no room in my head for anything negative. A soft glow shrouded every thought, every rationalization and emotion. I had difficulty remembering the question.

"What will I do if I need a drink of water in the middle of the night?"

"Just whistle." His lips began to work their way down my neck, nibbling at my collarbone.

"I never learned how to whistle." Speech was becoming extremely complex.

"Maybe you could groan or something," Malone suggested.

I moaned his name. It was a hoarse little whisper that caught on the edge of my lips. "Like that?"

"Close enough."

It was another evening of firsts. I'd never made love with my leg in a cast or busted ribs before. Of course, I'd never broken my ribs or ankle before meeting Malone. If anyone had ever suggested the act, I wouldn't have believed it possible. But Malone elevated my cast on pillows and supported his weight on his wrists and knees. Only the important parts met. Later, I dropped into a deep sleep, wrapped tenderly in his arms.

In the morning he fixed me breakfast in bed, then ran off to stock my fridge. I figured out how to prop my cast on the garbage can beside my desk, and still work my computer. Malone stopped back on his way to the station to check on me. He brought a bunch of clothes with him, so he could spend the night, and take care of me when he got off duty. Neither one of us mentioned how serious things were getting.

Shannon Ripley called late Tuesday afternoon.

"Don't you return your calls anymore?" There was just a hint of exasperation in her voice. Or maybe it was jealousy.

Embarrassed, I glanced at my machine. The little red light was blinking rapidly. Who thinks about phone calls after the weekend I had? "Sorry, I got in late last night."

"From where?"

"Never mind. Do I have to play the tape, or are you going to tell what you want?"

Shannon sighed and exhaled deeply. Either she had lost track of which day it was or she was bending her cigarette rule. I know she doesn't smoke in public and the walls of her office don't give away her vice with a nicotine tinge. "Myerson called yesterday."

My book editor. "And?"

"He read your revisions." Another extended breath.

"Well, don't rush to tell me, Shannon." She could be exasperating when she wanted to be. "What did he say?"

"He loved them. He wants to know if you'll marry him."

I knew the last part was a dig. Myerson preferred men. It was one of the few things we had in common. "Maybe in another lifetime."

Shannon shifted gears. "How's the new one coming? The story about the patrol cops?"

I blushed. "I'm still doing the research."

"Seems to me you've been spending a great deal of time researching this project. That's rather unusual for you, Jamie. Could this have anything to do with your absence since Friday?"

What the hell. Shannon knew me well enough by now. "Yes. He's got everything to do with it."

"Tell me all about him, sweetie. I want to hear every juicy morsel there is. Start with his name."

I didn't want to do this. Not now. "His name is Malone. Look, Shannon, I really don't have time right now to go into detail. Later on, I'll tell you everything. I promise."

There was a snap of a lighter and another huff of air against the phone. Shannon must be chain smoking, wherever she was. "As long as it's a promise, Jamie. Give my best to Malone. Just the mention of his name gives me the tingles."

"I know the feeling. We'll talk on Friday."

"Try to have an outline ready. It's easier to sell if I know what's going to happen."

"Yes, Mom. I'll see what I can do."

"You can be such a smartass, Jamie."

"Yeah, I can. And the worst part is I seem to attract other smartasses."

I could hear her chuckling deep in her throat. "Touché. Call me Friday."

"Bye, Shannon."

"Ciao."

I summoned up the file on the computer and reread my notes. At the bottom where Kleinschmidt had left a warning, I quickly noted the strange encounter on Saturday with the girl who might have been Melissa Hatcher. Then I did something really stupid. I entered all my thoughts about the weekend with Malone. Not just the romantic stuff, but about the accident at the gravel pit and my dozing off in the warm tub. Don't ask me why. I said it was stupid.

.

CHAPTER SIXTEEN

Malone stayed with me for the first week. The cast restricted my movements, a form of plaster related bondage. Malone was very inventive in new ways to make our nightly sexual activity enjoyable. I awakened each morning to the warmth of his body wrapped around mine.

Early the second week, Malone poked his head in my office before leaving for work.

"How's it going, Jay?"

"Just hobbling along, Francis." I'd gotten back into the game of giving him a daily first name.

"Think you can get along without me tonight?" He stood in the hallway, reluctant to invade my space.

"Sure. Is anything wrong?"

"Just kind of miss my own place. Thought maybe I'd spend the night at home, if you think you'll be okay. I don't want to give you the wrong impression, Jay."

I stopped typing and looked at him. "And what impression might that be?"

"You know, about us living together. You gave me keys to your place, and I've been here every night since we got back from Boyne. I prefer to take things slow."

"That's the best way with me too, slow and easy. I'll be

all right on my own. When will I see you?" Today was Tuesday. I almost dreaded his answer.

"How about Thursday, before my shift?"

Inwardly I sighed. "Okay, but how about Thursday, after your shift too?" It was easy to become greedy when it came to spending time with Malone.

My favorite smile arrived, just enough to touch the corners of his eyes. "Sounds good. Call me if anything comes up in the meantime."

I batted my lashes at him. "That should have been my line, sailor."

He came over and gave me a kiss, soft and gentle on the mouth. "See you Thursday."

"I'll be here."

Confusion overtook my brain for an hour after he left. Part of me was glad to have my own place back again. No more guilty feelings over not sharing the last scoop of Guernsey's peppermint stick ice cream. Or about my lack of culinary talents. I like cream cheese, pickle and hot sauce sandwiches on dark rye, but it's an acquired taste, definitely not for the faint of heart.

But another part of me was a little sad. Playing house with Malone was enjoyable. It was also comforting to have his warm body sharing my bed. Curling up together against winter's chill had quickly become one of my all-time favorite pastimes. Something about the way our bodies naturally fit together made the thought of his departure much harder to accept.

Was Malone the guy I'd been looking for? Or was he a convenient stand-in until Mr. Right found me? That was one question I couldn't honestly answer.

Thursday was light years away.

* * * *

A week later, I went to see my own physician and have my body checked out. Vincent Schulte has been my doctor since I'd gotten out of diapers. I used him as a reference source when I want to kill somebody in a story and make it medically accurate. In many respects, he's a surrogate father figure. Doc Schulte has always been there to give thoughtful, unemotional advice.

Don't get me wrong. I'm still closer to Bert than any of my mother's husbands or boyfriends. But Doc Schulte has been around me a lot longer than any one of Vera's revolving spouses. A widower for over twenty years, he took more than a casual interest in me since my father passed away. He knows more about me than anyone else in the world, my mother included.

Doc Schulte is pushing sixty, but I could never tell from which side. He's got most of his hair left and a pair of busy gray eyebrows that draw your attention away from his tiny brown eyes. He's around six feet tall, but stoop-shouldered, probably from too many hours bent over patients. He's always neatly dressed in a starched white shirt and a bow tie. The ties are his trademark. He must own over a hundred of them. He was clucking his tongue at me over my physical condition.

"Jamie, you shouldn't be overdoing it. Your body needs rest to recover from the shock. Take some time off work. Keep that foot elevated and cut down on the walking."

"I haven't been walking on it, Doc."

He stopped probing my ribs long enough to look me squarely in the eyes. "You've always been a terrible liar. Your cast is badly scraped along the bottom."

He had me. "So I've been walking a little."

"Bull. You've been walking a lot." His concerned look melted into a grin.

"Gonna spank me for being bad?"

"I leave disciplinary actions to the parents. I know you're a fast healer, but you should still take it easy. Rest. You're not in training for a marathon."

"Okay, so I'll take it easy," I said, without much conviction.

Doc raised his eyes from my ankle without lifting his head. He briefly tried for a stern expression then gave up. "Gee, what a surprise, a stubborn redheaded female. That's very uncommon for this time of year. They usually migrate south for the winter."

"Way my luck's been going I'd get stung by a jellyfish if I headed south."

He prodded me some more while waiting for the x-rays to develop. The ribs were healing nicely and my ankle was almost back to normal. Doc seemed pleased. He persuaded me to discuss some of my current projects and offered a few suggestions for exotic murders.

"You need something more bizarre, something that won't turn up so easily at the crime scene. Something to make the readers think," Doc said.

"You make it too bizarre and you won't keep the reader engaged. Nobody wants a know-it-all coming in at the end of the story, pointing out teeny-little clues that normal people would overlook."

"Hey, you can still make it interesting. You take a pastry chef who kills off her cheating husband with a poisoned rhubarb pie. Or a chemist who smears a solution made from soggy cigarettes on an embezzling business manager. My personal favorite is oleander. It's a very pretty flower that's common in California, but it's extremely toxic. Or…"

"Geez, Doc. I hope you don't get this weird with all of your patients. You'll be scaring business away.

He gave me a leer worthy of Groucho and patted my knee. "That's what keeps the good patients in line."

"I'd hate to see what you tell the bad ones."

* * * *

After Malone stopped spending every night at my apartment, my concentration grew progressively worse. I finished the outline for Shannon and was trying to work on my cop story, but I kept getting distracted. A few stray thoughts couldn't be ignored anymore, so I switched off the computer and rolled over to my phone. I called the nearest gun shop and asked a few questions about permits and purchases. He suggested I come in to browse and ask my questions in person. I was getting cabin fever anyway.

I stumped my way down to my car and drove over. The weather had turned from cold to frigid, with temperatures hovering around twelve degrees. Petrified gray piles of snow lined every curb, making walking difficult even for the sure-footed, of which I was currently not one. It had taken me two trips around the parking lot to get comfortable driving with my left foot. Good thing the Honda is an automatic. Doc Schulte had given me a temporary handicapped sticker for my car. Knowing I could never sit still for long, at least I had the option of special parking privileges.

The guy I'd been talking to on the phone met me at the front door. He was shorter than me, with the bulky shoulders and arms of a body builder. Thick brown hair cut short and a small gold earring in the left lobe. His name was Tony.

"Are you looking for an automatic or a revolver?" Tony asked casually.

"Don't really know. What's the difference?" I pretended ignorance. He might offer a lot more information if given the chance to show his expertise. Most people love to talk about their work. Tony was no exception.

"Automatics are more popular. Lightweight, good action, capable of a lot more rounds than a revolver. Some hold as many as seventeen."

"What about that revolver?" I pointed at a small one in the glass cabinet.

"Good choice. 38 Smith and Wesson with a two inch barrel, it holds six shots. One thing about revolvers, they never jam. Always got another bullet coming up when you pull the trigger. Up to six anyway." His enthusiasm for his work was evident.

"What's your preference?"

"Beretta 93 R. 9 mm with a fifteen round clip. It's accurate as hell, and lightweight." Tony tapped the counter beside the one we were looking at A row of automatic pistols gleamed beneath the store's fluorescent lights.

"How do I go about buying one?"

"First you need a permit. You can apply for one here. It varies from city to city. As long as you don't have a criminal record, you should get it back shortly. Some places take as long as a month. Then you choose the gun and we go from there. Ever fired a pistol before?"

"Once. It was a big automatic. I don't remember the name."

Tony drew a revolver and a small automatic from the case and held them up before me. "Want to try them out?"

I looked around the display cases of the crowded showroom. "Here?"

Tony grinned widely, showing a neat row of clear braces on crooked teeth. "We've got a range downstairs. C'mon. Give them a try. You can't make a decision without firing them."

I shrugged. "What the hell."

To my surprise, there was an elevator behind a curtain we took to the basement level. Tony turned as we left the car and entered a locked room beside the elevator. A steel door across the hall was the only other exit. I waited, balancing on my cast. A steady popping noise was faintly audible from the other side of the steel door. He came out with two sets of headphones draped over his arm, and two pair of protective glasses dangling from his hand. Tony also carried two boxes of shells. I gimped along behind him through the steel door.

"Why the elevator?" I asked.

"Some of our regulars are handicapped. Wheelchair bound. This makes our facility more accessible for them. There's even a league for wheelchair shooters. They meet here twice a month and compete. We give them a discount on ammunition."

"You guys think of everything."

Tony grinned again. "Got to cover all the angles. I'd rather have them ripping hell out of a paper target than taking out their frustrations on the street."

"You won't get any argument from me."

The room was broken up into twelve little alleys, with wooden dividers between the shooters. Paper targets hung at various stages. About half of the stalls were in use. Tony passed me a headset and settled the other one over his ears. Then he led me to an empty stall.

I watched Tony efficiently load the revolver. He snapped the cylinder back into place and spun the chamber. This was more for my benefit than anything else. We put the protective glasses on and he handed me the gun.

"Stand with your feet apart a little more. It will help your balance." He stood behind my shoulder as I leveled the gun at the target. Gently I squeezed the trigger like Malone had shown me and watched the little gun roar to life. The paper target jumped as the bullet passed through.

"Not bad," Tony nodded. "Rock your hand back a little, to bring the barrel up. Not too much."

I did as he instructed and slowly squeezed off the rest of the shots. When the gun was empty, I handed it back to him.

"You're pretty good. Want to try the Beretta?"

I shrugged. "Might as well. Do you have a lot of women buying guns?"

He nodded. "A few buy them for protection, but a lot of them are getting interested in target shooting. We recommend if you're going to buy a gun that you learn how to fire it properly. Also, it's a good idea to practice with the gun often, so it feels comfortable to you. If you are buying the weapon for protection, it shouldn't be something you are afraid of or don't like to handle."

"Guess it's not just a macho thing anymore." I took the offered automatic from him and swiveled around toward the target. I noticed Tony hadn't worked a round into the chamber, so I deftly racked the slide as Malone had shown me.

"You've been watching too many movies," Tony said with a grin.

I steadied the gun with both hands and knocked off a few shots at the target. The automatic jumped slightly in my hand but it was easy to make the adjustment. I brought my eyes around to question Tony and he nodded.

"Go for it."

I emptied the gun into the target and handed it back. He knocked the empty clip out of the handle and laid it on the counter before me. Both guns sat there, patiently waiting. They looked harmless, despite what they were capable of doing.

Tony stepped back, and I caught a glimpse of something in the next stall. What I saw caught me so off guard I started to lose my balance. The plaster weight on the bottom of my leg was momentarily forgotten. Tony grabbed my arm as my crutches went out from under me. It was too little, too late. I ended up on my ass. But my eyes never left the next stall.

There was a black arm, leather clad arm holding a small revolver. The hand clutched the gun and fired it steadily, evenly spacing out the shots. A neat row of leather fringe dangled from the arm of the jacket.

"Let me help you up," Tony offered.

"Three weeks in this damn thing, and I'm still tripping over it." I took his hands and was surprised at how easily he lifted me to my feet. All those hours spent pumping iron had served Tony well.

"Decide on a piece?"

"I'll have to give it some thought." My mind was on the arm I'd seen sticking out of the next booth. I accepted my crutches and hobbled around the partition.

I don't know what I expected to see. Maybe the guy who had tried to kill Smitty would be standing there, wearing a 'I Hate Cops' tee shirt. What I did see when I turned the corner was enough to give me culture shock.

He stood there in profile, right arm extended like a gunslinger. I took the whole picture in while struggling to regain my composure. He wore jeans and boots. A heavy denim shirt was visible beneath the leather jacket. The jacket was trimmed in fringe along the sleeves and shoulders. He finished the rounds in the revolver and flicked open the cylinder with a nonchalance that only comes from plenty of practice. He tipped the gun up, letting the empty shells tumble to the floor. He turned to face me, bowing slightly, as Tony joined me at the end of the stall.

"Mr. Nakajima. How are you today?"

"Very well. Is something wrong?" The man smiled briefly, his almond shaped eyes darting between the two of us.

I was dumbfounded and could only shake my head. Tony bowed from the waist. "Please, do not let us interrupt your practice. My friend was merely admiring your jacket."

He beamed and inclined his head toward us. "It was a gift. They seem to be very popular here. We don't see clothing such as this in Japan." Nakajima loaded the revolver and turned back to the range. Tony and I headed for the door.

"The Japanese are some of our best customers. They find a great deal of pleasure in owning guns while they are here. Many of them compete in small tournaments. Nakajima practices several times a week. He's a hell of a shot. Do you know him?"

I shook my head. "He reminded me of someone else."

Tony trotted ahead of me and swung the steel door wide, giving me a chance to escape the noise of the range. We stopped by the elevator. He returned the headsets and the glasses along with the extra ammunition to the secure room. We rode upstairs in silence.

"What do I owe you for the bullets?" I asked when we were back on opposite sides of the display counters.

He raised a callused hand before I could dig my wallet out of my purse. "It's on the house, Jamie. If you do decide to buy a gun, I'll throw in a box of shells and a cleaning kit. Then I'll give you a lesson on maintaining it."

"Thanks, Tony. I'll be in touch." I flipped him a wave and hobbled back out to my car. My mind was reeling with information. Never for a moment did I consider the Japanese man to be a suspect in Kleinschmidt's shooting, but the way my heart had jumped just seeing his arm beside the partition was enough to bring the whole night back in vivid Technicolor. I sat in the car, trying to calm down.

And that's when things got even more confusing.

Coming out of the gun shop was a blonde in jeans and a brown suede leather jacket with fringe along the sleeves. Suddenly these jackets were popping up everywhere. I wondered if there was a sale I'd missed. Not likely. She carried a brown paper bag to a Ford Explorer and swung in behind the wheel. As she bounced across the parking lot, she passed within five feet of my car, and I got a good look at her. Melissa Hatcher. I slouched low in the seat and waited until she rounded the corner before stumping back inside.

"That was fast," Tony said with a grin.

"I thought I recognized somebody, a blonde girl, late twenties or so."

Tony nodded. "Melissa. She was picking up some target loads."

"What's that?"

"Rounds we repack for target practice. They're not as expensive as fresh rounds. She dates a cop. I guess they spend a lot of time at the range."

My eyes went to the elevator. "Here?"

"Once in a while. There's an outdoor range for everything from bow and arrow to rifles. I think they shoot there every week."

"So what did she buy? Shotgun shells?"

Tony flipped open a log book beside the register and ran his finger down the page. "Two boxes of .38 caliber and two boxes of 9 mm. Target loads all the way around."

"Do you know if Melissa is any good with a gun?"

He shrugged. "She's been at the range a couple of times when I was there, but usually she just hangs around and watches her boyfriend." His friendly manner stopped as if someone had put on the brakes suddenly. Maybe he realized he had said too much. "Why all the questions, Jamie?"

"Just curiosity, Tony. I'm always getting ideas for stories. The more details I can gather at the time one hits, the better chances I have for making something out of it." I adjusted my crutches and turned to go.

"Now that you mention it, I do remember her shooting out there once. She was using his revolver. I don't think she was too comfortable with the gun."

"Thanks, Tony."

CHAPTER SEVENTEEN

It could be coincidence. So Melissa knew how to fire a gun. Malone had taken me along to the range once too. Maybe it was a cop thing. The swooning female escorts her protector to witness his performance with a weapon. His accuracy could be a form of an aphrodisiac. So why did I have the feeling something was not as it should be? Maybe Ace Richmond, Private Eye would spot it, but I couldn't. Stuck in a mental rut, I spun my car out of the lot and drove to the state police post. Malone came out to greet me in the lobby when he heard my cast thumping on the floor.

"Hey, Jay." Even with a trooper watching from the desk, Malone bent down and kissed me. Suddenly I worried that Bert might be around.

"Hey, Malone. We gotta talk."

He looked at me, a frown darkening his face. "That sounds serious. My office good enough?"

"Sure."

A few moments later he leaned a hip against his desk and stared at me calmly. "This must be important if it couldn't wait until tonight."

I'd forgotten he was coming by after work. "It might be

very important. It's about the person who shot Kleinschmidt."

The smile vanished and his face grew dark and serious. "Jesus, Jamie, I thought you agreed to drop it."

"I've tried. Damn it, I've tried every day to leave it alone. But I just can't. It's like this voice that won't stop talking to me. I have to answer it to make it go away."

Malone pushed off the desk and went to the door. He closed it firmly, then came back and perched again. He was scowling when he spoke. "This isn't good. You're going to get people upset with me. I'm not supposed to be discussing criminal investigations with civilians."

"I'm not any civilian damn you, I'm your girl." His attitude was irritating as hell.

"Girl?" He looked like his face was going to crack.

"Whatever. Girlfriend, lady, woman, babe, lover, you pick whichever one fits the best. I'm not just some lame civilian who doesn't understand what the fuck is going on. I was a witness..."

"Don't swear."

"I'll fucking swear if I fucking want to. I didn't go to Sister Jubilation's Sacred Heart of the Rosary School. Swearing is part of the way I talk, and it is part of who I am." I realized I was close to shouting.

Malone shook his head in disgust. "Okay. Go ahead and swear. Just keep your voice down."

He'd gotten me so flustered I'd almost forgotten why I'd come here. I settled back in the chair and took a deep breath. "Damn it, Malone. Do you want to hear what I saw or don't you?"

Malone rubbed his chin. "Sure. Tell me about what's got you so excited."

"I saw Melissa Hatcher, wearing the same type of jacket as the person who shot Kleinschmidt. She was at the gun shop over on Six Mile Road, picking up bullets for the range. She bought two types of target loads, .38 caliber and 9 mm."

Malone shrugged. "So what?"

I smacked him in the shin with my crutch. "*So what?* Don't you get it? She could be the one who shot Kleinschmidt!"

He offered me the most condescending look I've ever seen. "Where did you come up with that theory? All you've got is a few coincidences. One, she owns a jacket similar to the one you saw the night of the shooting. Two, she was buying bullets. That doesn't mean she even knows how to fire a gun. That's all you've got."

"What do you mean, that's all?"

"Why would she do it, Jay? Why would she plug her own boyfriend? If it were a domestic dispute, why would she still be with him? You're reaching. There's no motive. What possible reason would she have for shooting Kleinschmidt?"

"Can't you go to the range and dig out one of her bullets? Ballistics could compare it with the slug that hit Kleinschmidt."

Malone shook his head slowly. "The back wall of that range is solid steel. Every slug turns into mush. Even if we could identify a bullet she fired, there'd be nothing left but a little lump of metal. No way to compare it with the other bullet."

"So you're not going to do anything about it?"

"No."

"Why don't you confront her? Ask her if she has a gun and bring it in for testing." I wanted to throw my crutches at somebody.

"We don't have probable cause. No judge is going to give us a warrant based on the information we have."

"Why not question her without a warrant?"

"If Melissa did have anything to do with it, do you honestly think she's going to voluntarily turn over her weapon for comparisons?"

"This really sucks, Malone. It sucks big time."

Malone got off the desk and squatted down beside me.

"Go home, Jamie. Concentrate on your writing. Work on an article. Watch a movie. Leave the detective work to us. There just isn't enough evidence to work with yet. Let the pros do their job."

"What about Melissa? Aren't you even going to tell the detectives about her?"

Malone closed his eyes and drew a deep breath. "If I do, will you promise to go home and forget about this?"

"Yes. For today anyway."

Malone opened his eyes and smiled thinly. "Best I'm going to get out of you."

He helped me out of the chair. "Still coming to my place after work, Sylvester?"

"Still want me to come by?"

I nodded. "I'll warm your side of the bed."

* * * *

I didn't have an appointment but I went to Doc Schulte's anyway. The nurse looked at me funny, then went back to check with the old sawbones. She came out and waved me back after a couple of other patients had been seen. The others in the waiting room looked ready to lynch me. Doc kept me waiting a few minutes in exam room three, with nothing to look at but a cheap copy of a Norman Rockwell print. At last he came in, tiny brown eyes dancing under those bushy gray brows.

"What brings you by, Jamie? Any trouble with the leg?"

"In a manner of speaking. Can we take the cast off today?" I sounded like a little kid, afraid of getting a vaccination.

"Why the rush? It should stay on for a few more days."

"C'mon, Doc. I'm a fast healer. You said so yourself. The ribs are fine and the ankle wasn't a compound fracture. I'm dying to get this plaster off."

Schulte sat on the exam table beside me and toyed with his stethoscope. "I'd hate to remove it early and see you have a relapse. Then you'd have to start all over again."

"How about if we wrap it in an elastic bandage for a week or so? At least then I could wear some shoes. C'mon, Vince." I gave him my best 'lost puppy' look, lots of big eyes and lashes fluttering. "Please."

He always melted when I called him by his first name. He knew further discussion was pointless. "What the hell. But you have to promise to take it easy."

Suddenly I realized where I'd picked up my favorite saying. "Scout's honor," I said, holding up two fingers.

"You were never a scout." Schulte slid off the table and lifted my leg to examine the plaster.

"So sue me."

"Never say sue to a doctor. It makes him nervous."

When he sawed the cast off, I remembered I didn't have a shoe with me for that foot. I'd been expecting him to insist on leaving the cast in place for another week. I traded him my crutches for an old woolen sock to cover my toes after he wrapped my ankle in elastic. Vince helped me down, and I planted a kiss on his forehead.

"You're a prince."

He touched his head in surprise and smiled. "Just don't make me look like a fool for letting you talk me into this. My nurses will never let me hear the end of it if you end up in plaster again."

I gave him a tissue and pointed him toward the mirror. They would tease him forever if he didn't get the lipstick off before he left the room. Luckily, I'd been able to park near his office door. I made it through the snow without falling and slid behind the wheel of my car. Once home, I knew exactly what I had to do. A scalding hot bubble bath with lavender salts. I had no idea how badly my foot and leg would smell after being covered in plaster for three weeks. Phew!!

Afterwards, I put on flannel jammies and my heaviest robe and sat on the sofa. The Jewish Aunt sucked me down until only the top of my head would have been visible. I could look out at the treetops and the early evening streetlights.

Maybe I need a change. I've been living in this apartment damn near forever. Boredom was setting in. There was enough in the bank to make a nice down payment on a house, yet I never pursued the idea. Something about a single woman with her own home makes me think of a spinster, surrounded by cats. Not for me. But I could rent one, maybe for six months or a year. Give up this place, get into something bigger. Maybe even something with room for two, just big enough for Malone and me. As if on cue, the phone rang.

"Hey, Jay."

"Hey, Sylvester. I was just thinking about you."

He chuckled softly in my ear. "Are you naked?"

"Dream on, lover. Still coming by tonight?"

"If your invitation is still good."

"Absolutely. Want me to make dinner?" I could practically hear his stomach groan in protest.

"No, I won't last until then. I've got a meal break coming up soon. I'll grab a burger with one of the guys. See you around twelve."

"I'll be here."

I took some leftover pizza from the freezer and warmed it in the oven. I wondered what Malone would say if he knew what I'd been thinking. Living together was a common occurrence. Most people nowadays do it at some time or other. And most people end up getting married or breaking up. But that didn't mean we couldn't try. The worse that could happen would be Malone running away. Fast. I'd probably give up and join a convent. Something appropriately named, like 'Our Lady of the Perpetually Hopeless Relationships' or maybe 'Queen of the Hopeless Romantics'. But was I hopeless? I always thought of myself as hopeful. And Malone certainly could be romantic.

Malone came in a little after twelve. I was reading an

old Travis McGee novel in bed, snuggled down under the blankets. There was a pile of pillows around my foot to simulate the cast. He came into the room, still wearing his jacket, and flopped on the covers beside me.

"You're freezing," I gasped as he kissed me.

"Wanna help warm me up?"

"Only if you take off your boots first. I don't want snow on my sheets."

"No spirit of adventure."

He slid from the bed and quickly peeled off his clothes. I raised the covers a fraction to let him inside where it was warm. Out of habit, he avoided my right ankle. I slid my foot up his leg while he was busy kissing me.

"You're warm."

"One of us had better be. Why are you so cold, Sylvester?"

"I stopped to help a lady change her tire."

"That sounds pretty chivalrous. How young was she?"

Malone stopped kissing and looked up toward the ceiling. "Late sixties. She was on her way home from a late night bingo party. She had over eighty dollars in winnings on her."

"Did she offer you a tip?" I teased.

"She said my good deed would be richly rewarded." He paused and ran his hands down my legs. "You got your cast off!"

He leaned back to look at me, gingerly tracing his fingers down my leg, across my ankle. He was giving me shivers and it wasn't from the cold. "I bribed the doctor."

"What kind of bribe?"

"I told him he'd be richly rewarded.

* * * *

Late Friday morning, Malone went to the gym while I tried to get some work done. I kept thinking about the gun shop and finally made a decision. Tony caught the phone

197

on the second ring. He remembered me immediately.

"How long would it take for me to get a permit to purchase?"

"If you're a city resident, without a criminal record, you can fill out the paperwork today. It takes at least a week for the approval to come back. Did you decide on a gun?"

"The Beretta. Can we do this over the phone?"

He laughed. "No way. I can hold the piece for you, but all the paperwork is supposed to be done in person."

I told Tony I'd stop by later on and provide all the pertinent information for the permit. Since I'd never had anything more serious than a parking ticket, he didn't think I had anything to worry about. I went by the post office and the deli for lunch then swung by the gun shop. Tony helped me fill in the paperwork and showed me the weapon. We went down to the target range and I fired off another two dozen rounds. He explained the proper way to break down the gun and how to clean it.

Tony recorded the Beretta's model and serial number on the permit form. He then locked the piece in a vault with a tag on it. Once I got the permit, I could pick it up. He reminded me that when I transported it home, I would have to lock the weapon in the trunk. Otherwise, it wasn't legal. My permit only allowed me to own the weapon. A separate, more difficult to obtain permit is necessary to legally carry a concealed weapon.

As I was driving home, I passed a row of realty offices. It started me thinking again about renting a house and wondering how Malone would feel about it. I had a hard time fighting the urge to stop at one and see their listings. Instead, I picked up the local paper before going back to my apartment.

The ads were full of houses for sale and some of the prices seemed reasonable. But the idea of a permanent home still rocked me. The apartment had begun to shrink lately. I wanted more than this place, but not that much more. There was a short column with rental properties available. I pushed thoughts of guns and bullets from my mind and went to look at the houses in the paper.

The first two were duds. Tiny wooden square buildings, with as much personality as residential road kill. Maybe apartment living wasn't so bad after all. I kept going. The third one was a mansion, big enough for a football team, with a separate wing for cheerleaders. But then I saw the fourth one. Ah, now we were getting somewhere.

It was a ranch house. Brick, maybe forty years old, with a gigantic pine tree in the front yard. Real wooden shutters guarded the picture window facing the street. The house was in the middle of a block where no two homes looked exactly the same. Even from out in the street, I knew this was the place for me. I drove slowly away, dialing the number on my cell phone. The number turned out to be a realtor named Maybelle Ross. I asked her for the particulars on the house but she demurred. Her voice was sugary sweet, like Vermont maple syrup.

"I like to let the house speak for itself. Can you be there in ten minutes?" Maybelle asked.

"I'm just around the corner." She hung up as soon as I said it.

Maybelle Ross could have been anyone's grandmother. Snow white hair in tight little curls bounced on her head. Wide green eyes so merry, you expected her to pinch your cheek. She was shaped like a beach ball and seemed perfectly content that way. I could easily picture her wearing a frilly apron and pulling oatmeal cookies out of the oven. She left her Cadillac in the driveway and practically bounded across the lawn.

The house was even better on the inside. Originally it had contained four small bedrooms, a living room and a kitchen. There was a fireplace, a small yard in the back and a basement big enough to hold a bowling alley. Someone had knocked out the adjoining wall for two of the bedrooms and made it into a suite. There were hard wood floors throughout the place. The kitchen had a skylight over the workplace by the stove and sink, with a chopping block counter in the center of the room. A bay window looked out over the back yard. I was hooked.

I rarely do something on impulse. Usually I hem and haw, and scuff my toes in the dirt until someone else makes a decision for me. Especially on a decision that was something this big. But today was different. I was ready for action.

"How much?" My voice trembled as I asked.

Maybelle gave me the price. It was hardly more than I was paying for the apartment. "You pay your own gas, electric and phone. The landlord will take care of landscaping and snow removal, along with any repairs."

"How long has this place been available?" I was trying hard to disguise my excitement.

"Only a month. The woman who owns it is in a nursing home. Her son doesn't want to sell as long as she's alive, but he's willing to rent it," Maybelle said reassuringly.

"I'll take it." Somehow my checkbook had appeared in my hands. What was I saying about indecision?

Maybelle gently patted my hand. "Not so fast. We need to do a background check on you, before we agree to the rental. How soon would you like to move in, if everything is approved?"

Pretty soon they'll be doing background checks if you want to have a pizza delivered. "Next week?"

She grinned. "Just in time for Christmas, huh?"

"You bet. Can we do it?"

Maybelle bubbled over with delight. "Let's get started."

I followed Maybelle to her office and filled out a sheaf of silly forms. I wanted to spring it on Malone as a surprise, but I didn't know how he'd react. The place was big enough for both of us, yet affordable for me to rent alone. I wanted him with me, but didn't want to scare him away. I didn't know what to do. And I didn't want to think about Bert's reaction when he found out about Malone and me.

CHAPTER EIGHTEEN

The rest of the afternoon, I came up with different ways of springing the house on Malone. Every time I hit on something clever, I threw it out two seconds later as lame or immature. I had never lived with someone before. There was an edge of permanence to this that both excited and scared me. Would Malone want to move in? Would a trial basis be the best thing? Would he give up his own apartment, or keep it as a safe haven if I got too possessive?

The anticipation was driving me crazy. But then I realized something. I might not even get the house. I could be doing all this worrying for nothing. With an effort, I put it out of my mind and watched an old Bond movie. It was one of the originals, with Sean Connery as Bond, James Bond. He was so smooth, so suave. I relaxed and let him coax me into the movie.

It was after midnight when Malone crawled in beside me. Despite my attempts at staying awake, I'd succumbed to sleep an hour before. I made one decision during the movie. I was going to keep my mouth shut. At least until I knew the place was going to be mine.

Malone curled against my back and worked an arm

around my waist.

"Watch it, buster. My lover's a C.W.A.," I mumbled.

He nuzzled my neck. I could feel the faint scratch of stubble against my skin. "C.W.A. What's that mean?"

"Cop With Attitude."

"My kind of cop." His hand began tracing circles across my stomach.

I rolled over and snuggled close. The shapes were now being drawn on my tailbone and along my spine. "I was sleeping soundly until you came in, Merlin."

"Guess you're wide awake now, huh?"

"Does that mean you're not going to let me go back to sleep?" I smothered a yawn in his chest.

"Later. You can sleep until noon." Malone twisted onto his back and pulled me on top of him.

"Do you have any idea how romantic it is for a girl to be awakened from a slumber this way?"

"I'm a cop. I just respond to the clues and follow my instincts."

"Why, Merlin, whatever do you have in mind?"

He drew my face down to his. "It ain't step aerobics, but it should get your heart thumping."

I pressed his hand against my chest. "It already is."

Keeping quiet about the house was easier than I thought. It was Malone's turn in the rotation for a long weekend off. He had Saturday through Tuesday free. The idea of returning to Erhardt's chalet was appealing, but my ankle throbbed at the mere thought of outdoor activities. It was too close to Christmas to think about spending any more time wrapped in plaster. Outside the wind was screeching as the mercury dropped into the single digits.

Malone had other ideas. He left my place before noon and was secretive as hell. I couldn't go with him. All he said was to stay close to the phone and relax. That's easier said than done.

I was at the computer keyboard when he called an hour later.

"Hey, Jay."

"Hey, Merlin. What's going on?"

"All in good time, Jay. What are you working on?" He could hear the keys clicking in the background.

"Same old stuff, like trying to figure out a new way of killing somebody. Why?"

"Wrap it up and store it until Tuesday. We're leaving."

"I can't go out and play in the snow, Merlin. It makes my nose run."

"No arguments. Finish up. I'll be back in ten minutes."

"You're being awfully demanding this morning, Merlin."

"I'm a cop with an attitude, remember?"

"Touché."

I saved the file and shut down the system. Whatever he was up to must have something to do with his time off. I paced for a few minutes then sprawled on the Jewish Aunt. Maybe Ace Richmond, Private Eye could figure this one out.

It was half an hour before Malone returned. He insisted I stay in the living room while he packed a bag of my clothes. I was only allowed to collect a few toiletries and stuff them in a duffel bag.

"Grab your coat."

"Where are we going, Merlin?"

He hugged me. "Stop asking questions and come along."

"I don't like surprises."

Malone burst out laughing. "You're a lousy liar, Jay. Do you trust me?"

I realized I did trust him more than anyone else I knew, except for Bert and Doc Schulte and Shannon. But then like the Grim Reaper in some old movie, something else went flittering across the back of my mind. Images of a dark Malone flooded my brain. Here he was hovering above the tub in Erhardt's hotel. There was another one of him knocking me into the gravel pit. Which ones were real? I forced them aside. "Mostly."

"Someday I'll get you beyond 'mostly', but that's good enough for now."

He got me into the Cherokee and we headed down the road. We ended up at the airport and carried our bags inside. By the time we were heading for the boarding gate, it was evident where we were going. Miami. Who needs Ace Richmond? Malone wouldn't answer any questions until we were airborne.

"It's a package deal. One of the guys was going to take his wife for a long weekend. But she can't get the time off work and they couldn't get a refund. So I bought his tickets."

"What did you pack, Merlin?"

He shrugged. "I packed for you one cotton dress, blue and white, two pairs of shorts, two tee shirts, a red bikini and a tank suit and one pair of sandals. You're wearing jeans. That should do it. Oh, and a summer nightgown. Anything else you need, I'll buy it when we land in Miami. We'll rent a car and drive down to the keys."

I sighed. "That's not a bikini, you moron. It's underwear. You're pretty sure of yourself, copper."

"You know us cavemen. We take what we want. Three days in the sun, Jamie. Lean back and enjoy it."

"I certainly will.

* * * *

We came home late Tuesday, slightly pink and very relaxed. Nothing like seventy- two hours of the four S's to recharge my batteries. That's sun, sand, sex and seafood to you, although not necessarily in that order. We discovered some new places to make love, including a secluded beach and a hammock outside the bungalow we rented for a night. Then there was the outdoor shower stall and the tidal pool. We were very relaxed when we returned to the frozen north.

Wednesday morning I attacked the computer with new energy, my secret about the house intact. Malone went to the gym and then to work.

Maybelle Ross called with the news. My application to rent had been approved. I was excited and frustrated in the same breath. Where the hell was I going to find a moving company on a week's notice? I still had to notify my landlord that I was moving out, and would undoubtedly lose two month's rent on my lease. So what! I spent the rest of the day calling movers all around town. No chance. Everyone was booked until after the holidays.

I really wanted to spend Christmas in my new place. Part of the magic would be to spring it on Malone as a holiday surprise. Disappointment was closing in. I knew it was a last minute decision, but I had to go through with it. Inspiration saved me.

I didn't have to move completely, just enough stuff to get through a few nights. Kitchen gear for cooking, clothes to wear, gifts for the tree. A tree! Not some polyester conglomeration of wires and bristles. I wanted an honest to God Scotch pine with needles and a thirst, tinsel and popcorn and ornaments and lights. It was time to get moving.

I am notoriously bad at keeping secrets, but I was determined to hide this one from Malone. It turned out there was plenty for me to do to keep busy. Malone was pulling extra duty with the holidays so close. Other than time spent in bed, we hardly saw each other. Most nights were a marathon of sex. Occasionally, we did sleep.

My permit to purchase a gun came through without a hitch. I called Tony, brought the necessary paperwork to him, and went to pick up my new Beretta. Once again Tony convinced me to return to the range and practice. He said the more you use a gun, the more comfortable you become with it. I went through fifty shells while getting pointers from him. After the first three clips had been fired, he noticed I was dawdling

"What's going on, Jamie?" He touched my elbow while I was halfway through the fourth clip. There was no one else on the range.

"I need a favor." Up until that moment, I didn't know if I'd have the nerve to say it out loud.

"Like what?" Tony folded his arms and leaned back against the divider, his protective earphones draped around his neck.

"The woman I saw here that first time. Melissa Hatcher."

"What about her?" Tony wasn't going to make this easy.

"I want to try something, for a plot in a book I'm working on," I lied. "Can you get me a bullet fired from her gun? The .38?"

"What in the world for?" Tony relaxed a little.

"I've got this idea about framing somebody for a murder, but the key to the story is to gain access to their weapon. The bullet has to be identifiable. A slug from the back wall wouldn't work. It would be in no shape to match with the slug from the murder. I need a good clean specimen. How do I do it?"

Tony frowned thoughtfully then tugged at his earring. "Could be done, but it's not going to be easy. I could offer to clean the piece for her after she's been here. But it's doubtful she would go for it. Her boyfriend is pretty handy with his weapons."

"Is there some other way?" I tried hard not to beg. I didn't want to arouse his suspicions. This was supposed to be fiction.

"I could offer to mount a new scope on the gun for her. Her boyfriend has been trying to talk her into shooting in a tournament next month. Maybe I could get the gun from her then, and get a bullet."

"Great. But how can you fire a shot and still recover a usable slug? Remember, I need it good enough for the police to match it with the evidence from the murder."

"No problem," Tony said. "I'll use a test fire barrel."

"What's that?"

Tony smiled. "A test fire barrel. You shoot the gun into a metal drum filled with cotton padding. The density of the cotton absorbs the slug before it can travel all the way through to the other end of the drum. Then you have a clean slug to compare it with."

I was still skeptical. "How will you get a sample off of Melissa's gun?"

"I'll offer to mount the scope for her to try. While I'm working on it, I'll squeeze off a test round. With luck, I can persuade her to leave it overnight, so I can do the work and sight it in for her. Then she can practice with it before the tournament. She'll probably accept it as a free trial."

I fought the impulse to do a victory dance. "Great. Will you call me when you've got the sample bullet?" It was an effort to keep my voice calm.

Tony shrugged. "Sure. But why do you need one from her gun? Why not use one from another weapon?"

"She gave me the idea when I saw her buying the bullets." I gave him my best weak female look. Tony wasn't buying it. "I'm superstitious. If I can get an actual bullet from her gun, then the story will work out. If not, then there's no point in pursuing it."

"Guess it won't do any harm. I'll call you when I get the slug. She'll probably be in sometime this week. The outdoor range closed for the winter. We get a lot of their regulars practicing here until it warms up outside."

"Thanks, Tony."

"It'll cost you, Jamie."

I hadn't expected to get away with it for free. "Name it."

"If it does become a story, can you give me an autographed copy?"

"Hell, Tony, if it works out, I'll mention you as a resource. Your name will be on every book. And I'll pay for you to do the work on Melissa's gun."

His face split with a wide smile. "Great."

I went back to the apartment. After entering my conversation with Tony into the file on the computer and my ideas about where it might lead, I hesitated. Without meaning to, my story about the patrol cop was taking on a whole new direction. I pushed it away and concentrated on some revisions for a short story I'd been toying with. Malone was supposed to come by tonight after work. The afternoon passed quickly as I made my final adjustments to the story. I was debating about ordering a pizza or running out for a burger when my phone rang.

"It's Tony." He sounded nervous.

"You didn't change your mind about helping me, did you?"

"No way. I've got the slug."

I jerked back in surprise. "So soon?"

"Melissa and her boyfriend came in about an hour after you left. It took some convincing, but they finally agreed to let me keep the revolver to put the scope on. They're coming back in the morning to pick it up."

I checked the clock above my desk. Six forty-five. "Are you closed for the evening?"

"We shut down at six. I'm on my way home. I didn't want to call you from the store. One of the other guys might have overheard me."

"Can I meet you somewhere?"

Tony paused. In the background I could hear traffic going by. "Ever been to the Dizzy Duck?" he asked at last.

"The rock and roll bar on Haggerty?"

"Yeah, I'll meet you there in ten minutes."

Could it really be that easy?

* * * *

It took me fifteen minutes to find the place. I don't frequent many bars and I'd confused it with another one nearby. As I approached, I saw Tony leaning against a car

208

in the parking area, looking around anxiously. The only spot I could find was at the far end of the lot. I parked and began walking toward him. There was a string of holiday lights above the cars, making them all shine. Plows had built up large mounds of snow around the lot, and the cold temperatures had frozen them all into icy bunkers. Tony saw me approach and pushed off his car. He walked to meet me, his arms swinging wide as he moved.

An old Dodge pulled into the lot. Tony glanced over as it came alongside him. We were still about forty feet apart. The car was filled with four rowdy guys, bellowing out the lyrics to "Bohemian Rhapsody". As they passed between us, there were several catcalls and whistles directed at me. I waved as they crawled by and watched them look for a parking spot. When I turned back toward Tony, he was gone.

On the ground where he'd been standing was a crumpled lump, wrapped in a down jacket.

"Tony!"

I don't remember running or screaming, but apparently I did both. Kneeling beside him, I gently rolled him onto his back. Tony's eyes were staring vacantly at the string of lights. His neck had no pulse. If he was breathing, I couldn't tell. A first aid class from high school ran through my head as I began to check his body. While trying to open his jacket, I realized what had happened.

Protruding through his coat was a metal arrow about as big around as my thumb. Six inches extended from his chest. I screamed again and covered my face.

"Jesus Christ!" One of the guys from the Dodge appeared at my side and pulled me back a little. "Call the cops!" he yelled to his friends. "This guy's been shot."

Tears rolled down my face as I looked at Tony. This was my fault! Nobody else was supposed to get hurt. Yet here I was, kneeling beside someone I'd coerced into helping me. And now that someone was dead. Reaching out to take his hand, I felt a small cold lump. I rolled the slug into my palm and got to my feet. After making certain no one was paying any attention, I slipped it into my pocket and walked away.

Shooting Tony must have been easy. He was standing alone in the parking lot, near the one large streetlight. The rows of parked cars and the bunkers of snow would have provided excellent cover for someone to hide behind. The noise from the Dodge had been sufficient to mask a gunshot, let alone somebody using a bow and arrow. Other than the guys in the passing car, Tony had been the only one in the parking lot. Whoever killed him had slipped away amid the noise and confusion that followed. I felt ill.

I managed to walk back to my car. I didn't have the strength to drive, so I leaned against the hood and hugged my arms, staring at the motionless bundle on the ground. The local police arrived. They questioned everyone in the bar, trying to find someone who had seen anything. Eventually they made their way over to me. It gave me more than enough time to work on my story. Bert always said I think fast on my feet.

I lied. Told them I didn't have any idea why someone would kill Tony. Said I'd met him during the day at the gun shop where he worked, and he'd invited me to have a drink at the bar. That was all I could say. I kept my left hand jammed in the pocket of my jeans, maintaining contact with that nasty little slug. Was this what Tony had died for? Was it worth it? When the cops were done, I drove home. I was numb. Whether from the cold or the shock, I didn't know. I do know it was difficult to drive with the tears streaming down my face.

CHAPTER NINETEEN

Melissa and Kleinschmidt must have been suspicious about the whole thing. Maybe they had gone to pick up her gun and followed Tony. There was another explanation that I tried to ignore, but it wouldn't go away. Maybe the deadly little arrow had been intended for me. Not a comforting thought.

I paced the apartment, trying to decide what to do. Malone would know. I could take the slug to him and argue my way through his objections. Then ballistics could test it against the one that had injured Kleinschmidt. If they matched, I'd have all the answers. I grabbed the phone and called the post. Before they could answer I hung up.

What if Malone refused to help? An image of him pushing me at the gravel pit flared in my mind. On its heels was the memory of nearly drowning in Erhardt's tub with Malone's hands on my throat. Had he really been trying to pull me up, or hold me under? Could I trust him? Can you really trust someone you've known for such a short time? And there was something else I wasn't sure about. I'd never mentioned about seeing him stop on the trail between the slopes and the inn, talking to someone.

Maybe it *had* been Melissa. Maybe all those glimpses of him I'd seen being friendly and charming with others, like David Erhardt and Sean O'Leary, was just an act. Maybe he was involved.

"Malone. Can I really trust you? Can I even mostly trust you?"

Things couldn't have been spookier if he'd answered me. I grabbed my coat and bag and went back out to my car. Snow was starting to fall but I didn't notice it. I drove cautiously to the post and paced about the lobby until Malone came out.

"Hey, Jay." He bent down for a quick smooch. I turned away.

"Hey, Malone." I didn't know if my voice was as shaky as the rest of me.

"What's wrong?" He took my elbow and steered me down the hall to his office. I waited until he closed the door and repeated the question. "What's wrong?"

"I'm in trouble." My voice was a whisper. "I did something very stupid, trying to outsmart the bad guys. Now someone is dead."

Malone dropped to a knee in front of the chair I was sitting in. Gently he took one of my hands in his. "You're not making sense, Jamie. Slow down and tell me about it. Start from the beginning."

It took a lot of coaxing before I told him everything. I explained about meeting Tony and convincing him to help me get a slug from Melissa's revolver. About going to the Dizzy Duck, and finding him dead. Finally, I dug the bullet out of my pocket and handed it over with trembling fingers.

Malone turned it over in his palm and held it up to the light. He went to the phone behind his desk and punched up two numbers.

"Van Allen. Check the listing on the command board. I want whichever forensic guy is on call to come in and run a comparison for me....Ballistics....No, not in the morning, now, right now....Let me know when he's in."

He turned back to me. His voice was low. Malone spoke slowly, deliberately. Whether he was choosing his words carefully or trying to control his anger, I couldn't tell. "Go home. As soon as we know if it's a match, I'll call you. That was a hell of a risk you took, Jamie. This isn't some story you're making up. This is reality. You might have been killed. For all you know, they might have been aiming for you."

I got to my feet. "You think Tony's death at the bar was a coincidence?"

Malone shrugged. "I don't know what to think. Go home, Jamie."

I hesitated by the door. "Are you coming by tonight?"

"I don't know." Malone made no effort to see me out. He just sat there rolling the slug between his fingers, staring at the wall.

I drove slowly home through tears. Whether they were of anger or sadness, there was no distinguishing them. Thinking of Tony as I got out of the car reminded me of the Beretta still locked in the trunk. I slipped it in my jacket pocket and trudged up the stairs. At the landing for the third floor, I realized I hadn't locked the door on my way out. I'd been in such a hurry to see Malone, it hadn't seemed important. I let myself in and spun the lock behind me.

While everything was still fresh in my mind, I decided to get it down on the computer. What I really wanted to do was curl up in bed and cry, but I felt all cried out. If Malone came over or not, there was nothing I could do about it now. He had warned me about my obsession several times. Hell, way more than that. I'd blown it. The romance was over.

I felt chilled from the evening and huddled inside my jacket as I went into the spare bedroom. As I reached for the chair I noticed the glow on the computer. It was on.

The curse jumped from my lips in a snarl. "You

arrogant son of a bitch."

Behind me the closet door creaked open. Kleinschmidt stepped out and leaned against the frame.

"I told you to leave it alone," he mumbled.

He shook his head slowly and stepped toward me. He was wearing jeans and a heavy wool jacket. His right arm was in the sleeve but it hung limply at his side. "I warned you, Jamie, but you wouldn't listen. You're too damn stubborn."

Melissa Hatcher appeared at the door to the hall. She was in jeans and the fringed suede jacket, the blonde hair pulled back severely in a tight ponytail. Her face was strained. "You nosy bitch. If you'd left it alone, none of this would have happened."

"You killed Tony." My voice was hoarse. I was choking on my words, trying to contain my anger.

"You got him involved, Jamie. You killed him," Melissa said bitterly. She brought her arms up in front of her. In her hands was a miniature crossbow. It was shaped like a pistol, with a ten-inch metal arrow held in place by a taut bowstring. There was no tremble in her hands as she aimed it at my chest.

"Put it down, Missy," Kleinschmidt said.

"She knows everything. She'll ruin it for us."

Kleinschmidt stepped between us and put his hand out toward her. "There's a better way. We know she's accident-prone. She'll slip and fall down the stairs and break her neck."

I turned slightly and slid my hand into my pocket. The Beretta felt cold and heavy in my grip. Was it ready? Or did I have to rack the slide before I could fire? I couldn't remember how I'd left it in the trunk. How much time did I have? Would I be able to hold them off?

Did I have what it takes to shoot another person?

"Wise up, Melissa," I said. "Two murders in the same night with a crossbow are a little uncommon. You don't think the cops will make the connection?"

She glared at me. "There's no way to trace a crossbow. They sell these things all over town."

"Shut up," Kleinschmidt said.

"You and your damn snooping," she sneered, "why couldn't you just leave us alone?"

"I don't know. Witnessing Kleinschmidt getting shot must have had something to do with it."

"You weren't supposed to be there," she hissed. "He was supposed to be alone, just like every other night."

The frustration was evident on his face. "I tried to call you. How many times do I have to explain this?" Kleinschmidt reached his good hand toward Melissa. "It's gone too far, Missy. I never meant for anyone else to get hurt." She took a step back in the hallway, beyond his reach.

"You should have thought about that before Tony was killed," I said quietly. My hand tightened around the Beretta's grip. Loaded or not? Why the hell hadn't I waited at the station with Malone? Why did I suddenly do as he said, after weeks of arrogantly following my own path? Where did my stubborn streak go?

"I knew something was wrong since that day I saw you at the gun range," Melissa said. She shifted her gaze to Kleinschmidt. "I told you she was getting too close."

"You should have ditched the gun, Melissa, and the jacket. That's what started me suspecting you." I turned slowly in profile, keeping my right side hidden from view.

Her eyes were wildly dancing back and forth. "You never saw me. There's nothing to connect me to the shooting." She tried to line up the arrow with my chest but Kleinschmidt was still in the way.

"Your jacket will help. I'll bet somewhere along the back is a section of fringe missing. The forensic guys will match the pieces they found in the truck with your jacket," I said calmly. Gently, I eased my gun out and held it against my leg. Could I really shoot one of them?

"If you hadn't meddled, none of this would have been

necessary. Tony would still be alive. Nobody was going to get hurt." Melissa glanced back to Smitty. "Get out of the way. Let me finish it."

"No, Missy. We were only doing it for the money. You said we could retire on the pension and the lawsuit. But you never said anything about killing people." His voice had taken on a dead, wooden quality.

"It's not just fraud anymore, baby. We're talking murder. We can get away with it. I'll erase everything in the computer while you get rid of the body. No one will worry about her," Melissa pleaded.

"What about Malone?" I asked.

"Sarge won't forget about her that easily," Kleinschmidt agreed reluctantly.

"He told her to leave it alone," Melissa said. "We know that. He's probably pissed because she won't. Maybe he won't come around for a while. You know how stubborn he gets. We talked about it up at Boyne."

So it had been her! Malone had been my only hope of rescue. I couldn't believe I'd been so wrong about him. All this time, he was involved in the shooting. My mind went over the scenes of the weekend again. He had been trying to get rid of me! The bastard. I couldn't believe how devious he was. Maybe this whole romance had been simply his way of keeping tabs on me.

I'd had enough. My temper took over. Rage was boiling in my stomach, churning its way up my chest and my throat. He'd played me like a naïve patsy. I was just some stupid girl, swooning over the handsome cop and his romantic moves. That made me angrier than what Melissa and Kleinschmidt had done. I brought the gun up, and aimed it at Melissa's head. Hell, I'd had more than enough.

"Put the crossbow down." My own voice sounded cold and calculating. Ace Richmond, Private Eye had decided to join the party.

"She's got a gun." Kleinschmidt took a step toward me.

"You sorry son of a bitch," I hissed.

"Give me the gun," he said, raising his left hand.

"Herman, get out of the way!" Melissa screamed. His bulk was efficiently blocking her shot with the crossbow and he was directly in my line of fire.

"Give me the gun," he repeated, stepping closer.

"No fucking way!" He was only six feet away. If he lunged, he could yank the Beretta of my hand. I was through being subjected to this, being made a fool of.

"Give me the gun."

"Fuck you, Smitty." My hand tightened on the grip.

"Give me the..."

The roar of the Beretta interrupted any further argument.

Kleinschmidt crumpled on the floor, clutching his right thigh with his left hand. At the last second, I'd instinctively lowered the barrel while squeezing off a round. I'd been aiming at his knee, but my shot went high. As Kleinschmidt was falling, I caught a glimmer of movement from the hallway. An image of Tony with an arrow sticking out of his chest raced through my mind. I fell to my knees and rolled to the right, waiting for the dart to puncture my heart. My ears were ringing with the echo of the gunshot. In the distance, I could hear Kleinschmidt's groans from the floor.

The mind is a complex thing. Mine picks the strangest times to behave illogically. Right now, I'm trying to concentrate on survival, particularly my own. But important thoughts like where Melissa was and why hadn't she tried to play William Tell with my skull yet rambled through my skull. Yet the only thing my brain could focus on was Malone's soft voice calling my name. "Jamie, Jamie, Jamie..."

"Hey, Jay."

He was standing in the doorway, the little crossbow dangling loosely from his fingers. It was empty. Behind him was Trooper Rothman, squeezing Melissa Hatcher by the arms.

"Hey, Malone." My voice didn't sound so good.

"Put the gun down, Jay. It's over."

"Can I trust you, Malone?"

Disappointment flooded his face. "The hell kind of question is that? Of course you can trust me! You were right. Ballistics matched the slug from the crime scene. I tried to call, but your phone is out. I was afraid you might be in trouble."

"They were going to kill me, Malone." My legs weren't working. I realized I couldn't stand up.

"They tried, Jay." He pointed at the computer. The arrow from the crossbow had pierced the monitor screen. Shards of glass poked out from the cabinet as thin wisps of smoke rose toward the ceiling. Scratch one flat screen monitor. No warranty in the world covers violent attacks.

"Holy shit," I whispered.

"Damn right," Malone said. Behind him I saw Rothman put the handcuffs on Melissa and haul her out of the apartment. I was still on my knees beside my desk. "I'm sorry, Jay. I should have listened. I just couldn't accept the idea." Malone squatted down beside me and gently pried the Beretta from my fingers. Then he went down the hall and came back with a bath towel. He deftly ripped it into sections and used them to patch up Kleinschmidt until the ambulance arrived.

"Sorry, Sarge," he muttered. "It was never supposed to go this far."

"We're all sorry, Kleinschmidt." Malone shook his head sadly then looked toward me. "It's over, Jamie. It's finally over."

* * * *

Rothman returned with the ambulance attendants. They checked Kleinschmidt over and strapped him to a stretcher. His prognosis was better than the last time. Apparently the bullet had passed through cleanly and hadn't even nicked the bone. The medics were optimistic. He'd get stitched up and pumped full of antibiotics before Rothman carted him off to jail.

When they left I was sitting on my desk chair, pressing my hands between my knees to keep them from shaking. My eyes kept going back to the dark bloodstains on my carpet. Boy, there wasn't a chance in hell of getting my security deposit back by moving out before my lease was up. Now there would be a cleaning fee too.

Rothman cleared his throat. "Anything I can do, Sarge?"

"Give us a second, Marty." He removed the clip from my gun and racked the slide, ejecting the round in the chamber. Then he handed everything over to Rothman. "Make sure it gets logged in properly."

"You bet."

"We have to go in and file a report, Jamie. When that's over, I'll bring you home."

I was numb from the eyebrows down. "Whatever you say, Malone, but walking isn't going to be easy."

My favorite smile appeared. "I'll help."

At the station I told my version of the evening's events while Malone and Rothman listened. They kept the coffee coming and I drank enough to float a canoe before it was over. Trooper Van Allen came in with a report on Kleinschmidt. He was released from the hospital and was being held in the Plymouth jail, pending his preliminary hearing. Kleinschmidt would be charged with conspiracy to commit fraud, accessory to murder and attempted murder, among other things. The situation didn't look too good for him and Melissa. Van Allen left and a few moments later, Trooper Billings entered the conference room.

"That female you arrested is no newcomer, Sarge."

"What did you learn, Leo?"

"Melissa Hatcher's got a history of four arrests for confidence games, plus a misdemeanor charge of soliciting and one for possession of marijuana. Apparently she was able to persuade Kleinschmidt that once the governor laid him off, this would be his only way to get even. His career in police work would be over." Billings unwrapped two sticks of gum and worked them into his mouth.

"You talk to Kleinschmidt?" Rothman asked.

"He admitted everything. Claims he loves the girl. Melissa told him she'd leave if he didn't go along with her plan. She even had some sleazy lawyer preparing to sue the state and the department, for putting his life in jeopardy."

Malone shook his head. "She might have gotten away with it."

"None of us would have ever believed Kleinschmidt was involved in his own shooting." Billings said. "You guys all done here?"

"Yeah." Malone glanced at his watch then got to his feet. "Wait here while I change, Jamie. Then I'll drive you home."

I nodded and concentrated on my coffee. I didn't trust my mouth to do any work for me right now other than consume caffeine.

Before we could leave the post, Bert Nowalski arrived, bursting through the conference room door like a grizzly bear with his ass on fire. He didn't say a word, merely hooked a forefinger in my direction and led me to his office.

"Start talking," he grumbled, slamming the door behind us. "And you can save the big words. What in the name of Brenda freaking Starr is going on?"

I'd been dreading this confrontation. Surprisingly, I was able to summarize the whole thing in eight short sentences. "Kleinschmidt and his girlfriend staged the shooting. A lawsuit and insurance money to offset the layoff was their motive. I tipped to it when I kept bumping into them. They killed a guy who brought me a slug from her gun. Ballistics matched. They confronted me at home. I shot Kleinschmidt. Malone grabbed the girl."

Bert didn't say a word. He just kept staring at me. Then he seemed to absorb what I'd said with one deep breath.

"You okay?"

"Wobbly, but no wounds, if that's what you mean." I moved toward him and wrapped my arms around his back. He held me close.

"You scared the hell out of me, Jay."

"I'm sorry, Bert."

"Vera knows anything about this?"

I shook my head. "She's in Maui for the holidays. No need to spoil her vacation."

"When isn't she on vacation?" he muttered.

"It's easier this way. I like being on my own."

He moved me out to arm's length and looked me in the eye. "Probably shouldn't be on your own tonight. You could come to my place."

I blushed. "Actually, I won't be alone."

"You're dating again?" There was a hint of disbelief in his voice.

"For almost three months now."

He watched as my embarrassment darkened my face even further. "That's about the same time all this started. Are you telling me…?"

A knock on the door saved the day. Or so I thought. Malone poked his head in when Bert called out. Even from here I could tell that he was no longer in uniform.

"Sorry, Captain. Jamie, whenever you're ready, let me know. I'll be in the lobby." He quickly pulled the door shut.

Bert stared at me for a long moment. After the first few beats, I couldn't meet his eyes. He realized he was still holding me at arm's length. Bert relaxed his grip for a second then slowly pulled me back for another hug. Two hugs in the same night. I felt like a safe teenage girl the way he'd wrapped those paternal arms around me. The fact I no longer was an innocent young girl made me a little sad, on top of everything else. I gradually pulled back before I started crying again.

"Malone? Jamie, I thought you of all people would know better than to get involved with a cop."

I wiped a smudge of makeup off his cheek. "So what's wrong with cops? I can think of at least one I'm particularly fond of."

Bert rewarded me with that snort of laughter. "You're a piece of work, Jamie Rae. Malone's a good man. Probably the best cop I ever worked with."

I gave him a kiss then turned for the door. Inspiration struck as I opened it.

"Hey, Bert. What's Malone's first name?"

The face splitting smile returned. "Sergeant."

CHAPTER TWENTY

We were on the Jewish Aunt, with our feet propped up on the coffee table. Between my nerves and the caffeine, there was little chance I'd slow down before New Year's Eve. Malone even listened to my theory on how Kleinschmidt and Melissa had staged the assault.

"After the shooting, Melissa drove the pickup truck to the junkyard. She probably took a hunk of hamburger and filled it with sleeping pills or tranquilizers that you could get at a drug store. I'd guess three pills would be enough to knock out Brutus. He makes a load of noise, but he'll take food from strangers."

"You know that for a fact?" Malone asked softly.

"I fed him a piece of steak one night."

Malone rewarded me with a brief version of my favorite smile. "Go on."

"Okay. She drugs the dog then uses a pair of bolt cutters to get into the yard. The chain was cut recently and Joe had to replace it. She hides the truck way in the back, then walks out and closes the gate. There's a trail that leads back into the trees by the yard. I found tire tracks in there, which would probably match her motorcycle if the snow and frost haven't ruined them."

"I wouldn't count on those being any good now. So she and Kleinschmidt planned the whole thing." Malone shifted his weight and slid his arm around me. He pulled me close, then a little closer still. I didn't want to ever leave his arms.

"Melissa's a decent shot. She plugs him in the wing and disappears. Kleinschmidt tried to get through to her that night, when we stopped for dinner, but she was already gone. He knew she was inside the truck, which explains why he approached it so openly. Kleinschmidt was probably going to tell her they'd better wait, until he didn't have a witness riding with him. Instead she shot him before he could warn her."

Malone picked it up from there. "Kleinschmidt figured to draw his full pay until his wound healed. But when the complications set in, it was as if they'd won the lottery. If his injury ended his career, he'd draw two thirds of his pay, tax free, for life. That is a whole lot more money than he would have gotten from the governor's budget cut. Chances are if they had pursued a lawsuit, the state might have settled out of court if they thought Kleinschmidt had a case. It's anyone's guess as to how much they could have gotten away with. That's pretty devious."

"But why break in and threaten me?"

"Melissa knew how to handle the computer and she wanted to learn what you had seen at the shooting. If you weren't close to the truth, they'd forget about you. According to Kleinschmidt, Melissa was the one who insisted they pressure you."

I huffed out my cheeks. "The more they shoved, the madder I got."

"Never argue with a stubborn redhead." Malone held me tight and rested his chin on the top of my head.

"Some people never learn."

"Got to give you credit, Jay. You figured out the entire scheme and even came up with a way to prove it."

"Just call me Ace Richmond, Private Eye."

He started to slide down, to recline on the cushions with me in his arms. But I pulled away. There were some things I had to ask. "What about you, Malone? You met her at the ski lodge that weekend, didn't you?"

He made no attempt to move. "It was a coincidence. She saw me on the slopes during the last run and waited for me to finish up. Melissa pumped me for information about your research, but I couldn't tell her anything. She did ask me to keep you away from Kleinschmidt, and I promised to try."

"That's it?" I dreaded his answer.

"Yeah, that's it. What else could there be?"

I pulled in a deep breath. "What about the gravel pit. Did you push me, Malone?"

His face paled and those cobalt eyes grew wide. "You're crazy, Jay. The edge gave away beneath you."

"And what about the tub?" It hurt to ask, but I had to know.

Malone got up from the aunt. For a long minute, I thought I'd blown it again. He was going to pack up his clothes, his spare razor and the neon green toothbrush. Then he'd be gone. Instead he went into the kitchen and came back with a sharp carving knife.

"Jesus, Malone, *put that down*!"

"It's the only way, Jay. I'm sorry it came to this." He stood in front of the aunt and plunked the knife on the coffee table, the handle close to me. Then he pulled out his off-duty weapon and laid it alongside the knife.

"Malone, what the hell are you doing?"

He knelt on the opposite side of the table and extended his arms out, so he looked like an airplane about to take off. With an inclination of his head, he gestured toward the two weapons.

"Take your pick, Jay, knife or gun. If you really believe that I would do anything to hurt you. There's no way I could harm you."

"You're scaring me, Malone."

"C'mon, Jay. Think about it. You're a klutz. When you get preoccupied, you trip over your own shoes. You get dizzy turning a corner when you walk down a hall. We were having a great weekend up north. You moved too close to the edge. The snow gave way and down you went. I was nowhere near you. I was checking the snowmobiles to make sure they were secure. It was an accident, plain and simple. That's all it was."

My eyes kept flitting from the weapons to his face. He showed no sign of fear. If I really thought he had tried to hurt me, I could even the score in a flash. Either Malone was extremely trusting, or seriously nuts.

"I could never hurt you, Jamie, never."

"I love you, Malone. Honest to God, I do."

He picked up the gun. In a flash, the weapon was back in its holster. Then he reached down and pulled me off the sofa. "Okay."

"Okay? You scare the shit out of me and all you can say is okay!"

"Hush, Jamie.

"Here I am, thinking you were trying to kill me. Please don't hate me."

"Hush." He kissed me, gently finding my mouth with his. "I could never hate you, Jamie. I love you."

"That was a pretty drastic way to prove your point, Malone."

"Drastic circumstances call for drastic actions." He kissed me again and slid his lips around to my throat.

"Malone…"

"Hmm."

I grabbed his head and pushed it back so I could see his eyes. "You're making me drastic."

The low wattage smile was back. "Yes ma'am."

* * * *

Late the following afternoon Bert called. He invited

himself over to the apartment and I didn't object. Malone was gone to work his regular shift. He had helped me clean up the mess from the shattered monitor and we had used three cans of cleaner trying to get the blood out of the carpet. I had a feeling the landlord would replace it when I moved out. At least there wasn't the chalk outline of a body to deal with too.

When Bert came in he greeted me with a bear hug and didn't immediately let me go. I realized again how much I missed those parental embraces. I couldn't remember the last time Bert had been to the apartment. That was a shame. I promised myself right then to invite him over often when I moved into the house.

"How are you, Jamie?"

"Better. Some sleep helped."

Bert eyed the sofa suspiciously and opted for the rocker. I perched on the edge of the table. He turned down offers of coffee and tea.

"Do you remember when we talked about finding a balance?"

I nodded. "Sure. I think you said something about letting someone into my heart."

"Yes, I did. But I didn't mean that person should be a cop."

A smile crossed my face and I realized I was blushing. I also noticed how uncomfortable Bert was. I had never witnessed him being uncomfortable before.

"Why, Captain Nowalski. Are you insinuating that I let the circumstances of the Kleinschmidt shooting sway my judgment?"

"You're enjoying this, aren't you?" he said with a scowl.

"As a matter of fact, yes, I am."

"You couldn't find somebody else? Like an accountant or a baker or maybe a dermatologist? You had to get involved with a cop?"

With a laugh, I leaned over and kissed his cheek. "A dermatologist?"

227

He shrugged and shook his head. "Hey, it's what came to mind. I would think after spending most of your formative years with me as a stepfather, you'd steer clear of cops, just in general principle."

Scooting closer, I took both of his hands in mine. "Bert, you are the greatest guy I have ever known. On the outside, you're this tough grizzly bear. But on the inside, you are a kind, generous, caring man. If Vera weren't so crazy, she would have recognized what she had in you and would still be married to you. I am very fortunate to have you for my father."

"Stepfather," he said, making the correction.

I slowly shook my head. "Father. You're the one, Bert. No matter who Vera has married before or since. You're the father in my life. And you always have been."

He squeezed my hands and his head nodded ever so slightly. "Thank you."

"So, are you okay with me seeing Malone?"

Bert chuckled and climbed out of the rocker. "Malone's a good man, Jamie. I just wonder if he has any idea what kind of a woman he's getting involved with."

"I think he's finding out."

* * * *

Christmas Eve and Malone was scheduled to work a sixteen-hour shift. Some of the guys traded duty, to fit in with their family plans. Malone worked from noon until four the next morning. We would spend Christmas Day together, and he would go back on duty the following afternoon. It was tough, but I managed to wait for him to come home. He slipped into the apartment quietly and almost walked past me. I was curled up on the Jewish Aunt, only my nose visible.

"Hey, Roland," I whispered.

He jumped. "Hey, Jamie."

Malone slid beside me and covered my face with kisses.

After a while he sat up and started to unzip his jacket.

"Keep it on." I struggled out of the aunt.

"Why?"

"Because we're leaving, that's why."

"Where are we going?" His eyes were barely visible in the dim light from the window.

"It's a surprise. Trust me?"

There was a moment's hesitation. "Mostly."

Can you believe it? The guy was using my own line on me *again*. "Then shut up and follow me."

"There's nothing quite like a demanding woman."

In the car I handed him a blindfold and wouldn't start the motor until he'd slipped it on. After a little grumbling, he did as I asked.

"Kidnapping is against the law."

"You're too old to be a kid, Roland. I'll let you take the blindfold off soon, if you're good."

He sat there patiently while I drove to the house. It was only a few miles away and traffic was nonexistent. A light dusting of snow had fallen earlier, making everything sparkle. I parked by the curb and helped him from the car. He held my arm gingerly and followed me up the walk and the two short steps to the front entrance. Inside I made him stand by the door and wait. Only after I lit the fire in the hearth and turned a couple of switches on did I let him take the blindfold off.

"What's going on?" Malone blinked as his eyes swept the room.

"Welcome home, Roland." I patted the sleeping bag beside me. I was sprawled on top of another one, clutching my long, wool winter coat around me. A queen-sized air mattress was beneath them, giving the nest a bed-like quality.

"Home?"

"It's my new place. I rented it last week."

"Home?"

"Room for two, Malone, if you're interested."

He stood there by the door, staring. I couldn't read his reaction from here and started getting nervous.

"Aren't you going to come in?" I pleaded. "Take the chill off, get cozy."

In front of the picture window was our tree, five feet of Blue Spruce, trimmed with little lights, ornaments and strings of popcorn. Outside I'd wrapped the railing in tinfoil and red ribbons. The fire was burning strongly, throwing heat toward the sleeping bag nest. Beneath the tree were a dozen packages for Malone. Each one bore a different name.

"I don't know what to say, Jay." He spoke so softly it hurt my ears.

"Don't say anything, Roland. Just haul your ass over here. "

He peeled off his jacket and came to me. I tried to convince myself I was trembling because of the cold but even I didn't believe it.

"Aren't you going to take your coat off? It's warm in here." Malone knelt beside me and took my face in his hands.

I shook my head. "You do it. First present on Christmas Day."

Malone laughed when he realized what I was wearing beneath the coat. There was just a black satin negligee and my little Santa Claus earrings. Tenderly he peeled off my coat and boots and helped me slide beneath the warmth of the sleeping bag. I'd zipped the two of them together so we'd have plenty of room. I was surprised at how quickly Malone could get out of his clothes. It must have been the proper motivation.

"Jay, about this house..."

"Hush. Let's not talk about it until after the holiday. I want this to be a happy time. A day filled with lots of smiles and love and warmth. Okay?"

He moved against me and my body automatically reacted with his. It was as if someone had thrown a secret switch.

"Wanna start with the love and warmth?"

* * * *

It was late morning when I woke up. The fire was still burning brightly, jolly yellow flames jumping across the wood. Malone must have rebuilt it when he got up. The stack of birch logs in the brass stand I'd bought last week was down by half. I found my robe and padded into the kitchen, expecting him there. The place was empty. Coffee had been brewed and there was a dirty skillet in the sink. I found a plate in the fridge with my half of breakfast. Malone was gone.

"You did it again, Jamie. You drove another good man away faster than the Black Plague. Maybe you could set a world record for the most disastrous romances." I was so stunned I didn't realize I'd spoken the words out loud.

His presents were unopened beneath the tree. His clothes from last night were gone. I went into the shower as the tears began to fall. If they mixed with the spray, I could always claim I hadn't really cried. The house must have been too much for him. Words like freedom and independence and space flickered through my mind. At least he could have said good-bye. If nothing else, I deserved a good-bye.

I didn't get out until the water ran cold and my skin was beginning to wrinkle. All my plans for the day had revolved around Malone. I'd been hoping he would cook dinner. Cornish hens were in the fridge, along with the fixings for salads and dessert. I was going to try my luck at baking an apple pie. I dried off and went into the suite. Most of my clothes were hanging in the closet. Nothing appealed to me. I found the baggiest jeans I own, remnants from a time I was fifteen pounds heavier. A worn Miami Dolphins jersey topped it off. I didn't even bother drying my hair. I felt like screaming. So I did.

"Damn you, Malone! Why the hell couldn't you have stayed the night?"

"I had to take care of something."

I jumped when I heard his voice and ran down the hall to the living room. He was sitting with his back against the wall, watching the fire. Only now did I realize there was music on the stereo. I recognized the strains of "All I Want for Christmas is you." How appropriate.

"Malone." I threw myself on top of him and kissed his mouth, his cheeks, his eyes, and his nose.

"Hey, Jay," he said softly.

I drew back and raked my wet hair out of my face. Then I hit him, as hard as I could, with a fist on the chest. "You son of a bitch. Don't you ever leave like that again! How could you..."

"Whoa. Take it easy." His arms squeezed me tightly against his chest, forcing away my anger. "Didn't you read my note?"

"What note?"

"That note." He jerked a thumb at the tree. Hanging from a string of lights was a square piece of paper. I pulled away from him and crawled over to it.

Back soon have to help Santa with his delivery.

"Oh shit." I felt like an idiot. The base of the tree was now filled with brightly wrapped packages I hadn't put there.

"I had all your presents in the back of the Jeep. You were still sleeping, so I took your car back to the apartment to pick them up." Malone stroked my hair behind my ears. Will my emotions ever stop being on a roller coaster?

"Oh shit."

"You said that, Jay."

"I'm sorry, Christopher."

"Merry Christmas, Jay." He pulled me back to the sleeping bag nest by the fire and tugged the baggies off my hips.

"Merry Christmas, Christopher."

If there is anything more special than making love on Christmas Day, I've yet to discover it. And right there, with the warmth of the fire, the soft music accented with the snap of logs burning, it didn't matter if we were on a makeshift bed. It didn't matter that my hair was wet, that I had no makeup on. It didn't matter ten minutes ago I'd been in tears in the shower, doubting what Malone and I had. The only thing that mattered was that Malone was here with me now. Of all the presents he gave me that day, making love that morning was what I treasured the most.

Malone loved the house, especially the kitchen. He whipped up dinner after we'd shared a shower and opened our gifts. Mine all bore goofy tags as well: one for J.R., another for Jamie, one for Jay, even one to Ace Richmond, Private Eye. And the presents were proof that Malone paid attention. There was perfume, a sweater, two pairs of dangling earrings, some CDs, a couple of books, tickets to a play in Toronto and some lingerie that actually made me blush. And those were just the things I could remember.

While the hens were roasting, we took a walk around the neighborhood. Everyone had their decorations lit and the little bit of fresh snow made the scene look like a holiday postcard.

"You really like the house?"

"Absolutely, Jay. When are you moving in?"

"After the first of the year. I'll need to get a little more furniture, but nothing that won't wait until I'm settled in. One room is big enough for my office and the other will be a guest room. In case I ever have any overnight visitors."

"What about me?"

I shivered when he said that. "You can always sleep in my room."

"That's not what I meant. Were you serious last night about living together?"

I couldn't believe my ears, but couldn't resist the urge

to tease him. "Well, I don't know. I mean, could I really live with a guy who doesn't even have a first name?"

He stopped walking and pulled me around to face him. I was melting into those cobalt blue eyes when he leaned in to kiss me. I've never known anyone whose kisses tasted so good. Never before have I enjoyed how one kiss leads to another. I didn't want Malone to ever stop kissing me.

I have no idea how long we stood there kissing. I do remember hearing car horns blaring as someone went down the street. But I can't tell you about the car. Kissing Malone always makes my eyes go out of focus.

"I'm not trying to rush you, Jay. Just thought that since you've got so much space and all, maybe it would be a good time..."

"Yes, Christopher. I was hoping you would want to move in."

"You sure?"

"As sure as I ever get. Come live with me, Malone."

"Slow and easy?"

"One day, then the next. We'll just walk together, go slowly and see where this leads. No strings."

He linked his arm through mine and turned me back toward the house. One thing still bothered me, but it wasn't really important.

"Are you ever going to tell me your first name, Malone?"

"What's in a name, Jamie?"

I sighed. "Looks like I'll just have to keep guessing until I get it right."

He nodded. "It shouldn't be that hard for Ace Richmond, Private Eye."

We turned up the walk for the house. "I've cracked tougher cases."

THE END

ACKNOWLEDGMENTS

Special thanks to Kim Love, Joanna Huestis and Travis Love for proofreading my efforts and all their great suggestions.

MARK LOVE

ABOUT THE AUTHOR

Mark Love (yes, that's really his name) lived for many years in the metropolitan Detroit area, where crime and corruption are always prevalent. A former freelance reporter, Love is drawn to mysteries and the twists and turns that mirror real life. He is the author of "Why 319?" and three books in the Jamie Richmond Series "Devious" "Vanishing Act" and "Fleeing Beauty" and several short stories.

Love resides in west Michigan with his wife, Kim. He enjoys a wide variety of music, reading and writing fiction, cooking, travel, most sports and the great outdoors. You can find his blog at the link below and on Goodreads, Facebook, and Amazon.

http://marklove024.blogspot.com/
https://www.goodreads.com/author/dashboard
https://www.facebook.com/MarkLoveAuthor
http://www.amazon.com/-/e/B009P7HVZQ

13509849R00142